PENGUIN CLASSICS

THE SHORT REIGN OF PIPPIN IV

Born in Salinas, California, in 1902, JOHN STEINBECK grew up in a fertile agricultural valley about twenty-five miles from the Pacific Coast—and both valley and coast would serve as settings for some of his best fiction. In 1919 he went to Stanford University, where he intermittently enrolled in literature and writing courses until he left in 1925 without taking a degree. During the next five years he supported himself as a laborer and journalist in New York City, all the time working on his first novel, *Cup of Gold* (1929). After marriage and a move to Pacific Grove, he published two California fictions, *The Pastures of Heaven* (1932) and *To a God Unknown* (1933), and worked on short stories later collected in *The Long Valley* (1938). Popular success and financial security came only with *Tortilla Flat* (1935), stories about Monterey's paisanos. A ceaseless experimenter throughout his career, Steinbeck changed courses regularly. Three powerful novels of the late 1930s focused on the California laboring class: *In Dubious Battle* (1936), *Of Mice and Men* (1937), and the book considered by many his finest, *The Grapes of Wrath* (1939). Early in the 1940s, Steinbeck became a filmmaker with *The Forgotten Village* (1941) and a serious student of marine biology with *Sea of Cortez* (1941). He devoted his services to the war, writing *Bombs Away* (1942) and the controversial play-novelette *The Moon Is Down* (1942). *Cannery Row* (1945), *The Wayward Bus* (1947), *The Pearl* (1947), *A Russian Journal* (1948), another experimental drama, *Burning Bright* (1950), and *The Log from the Sea of Cortez* (1951) preceded publication of the monumental *East of Eden* (1952), an ambitious saga of the Salinas Valley and his own family's history. The last decades of his life were spent in New York City and Sag Harbor with his third wife, with whom he traveled widely. Later books include *Sweet Thursday* (1954), *The Short Reign of Pippin IV: A Fabrication* (1957), *Once There Was a War* (1958), *The Winter of Our Discontent* (1961), *Travels with Charley in Search of America* (1962), *America and Americans* (1966), and the posthumously published *Journal of a Novel: The* East of Eden *Letters* (1969), *Viva Zapata!* (1975), *The Acts of King Arthur and His Noble Knights* (1976), and *Working Days: The Journals of the Grapes of Wrath* (1989). He died in 1968, having won a Nobel Prize in 1962.

ROBERT E. MORSBERGER, PH.D., University of Iowa, is former department chair and professor emeritus of English at California State Polytechnic University, Pomona. He served for two years as a visiting professor at the University of Nigeria and was a seasonal ranger/historian for eight summers with the National Park Service. His ten books include the first book-length study of James Thurber, two volumes of *American Screenwriters* that he coedited for the *Dictionary of Literary Biography, Swordplay on the Elizabethan and Jacobean Stage,* and *Commonsense Grammar and Style.* A John Steinbeck specialist, he edited Steinbeck's screenplay *Viva Zapata!* for Viking/Penguin and has published hundreds of articles, stories, and reviews.

KATHARINE M. MORSBERGER, PH.D., University of California, Riverside, was director of publications at Pitzer College and has taught at the California State University, San Bernardino. An eighteenth century specialist, she has published numerous articles and reviews, most notably in *Studies in Eighteenth-Century Culture* and *Pacific Coast Philology.* In collaboration the Morsbergers published a biography, *Lew Wallace: Militant Romantic,* several articles on Steinbeck, a chapter on Christopher Isherwood's *Frankenstein; The True Story* and another on "Robin Hood in the Movies," and an introduction to the Viking/Penguin edition of Johnston McCulley's *The Mark of Zorro.* Both Morsbergers are drama reviewers for the *Claremont Courier.*

JOHN STEINBECK

The Short Reign
of Pippin IV

A FABRICATION

Introduction by ROBERT MORSBERGER
and KATHARINE MORSBERGER

PENGUIN BOOKS

PENGUIN BOOKS

Published by the Penguin Group

Penguin Group (USA) Inc., 375 Hudson Street, New York, New York 10014, U.S.A.
Penguin Group (Canada), 90 Eglinton Avenue East, Suite 700, Toronto,
Ontario, Canada M4P 2Y3 (a division of Pearson Penguin Canada Inc.)
Penguin Books Ltd, 80 Strand, London WC2R 0RL, England
Penguin Ireland, 25 St Stephen's Green, Dublin 2, Ireland (a division of Penguin Books Ltd)
Penguin Group (Australia), 250 Camberwell Road, Camberwell,
Victoria 3124, Australia (a division of Pearson Australia Group Pty Ltd)
Penguin Books India Pvt Ltd, 11 Community Centre, Panchsheel Park, New Delhi – 110 017, India
Penguin Group (NZ), 67 Apollo Drive, Mairangi Bay, Auckland 1311, New Zealand
(a division of Pearson New Zealand Ltd)
Penguin Books (South Africa) (Pty) Ltd, 24 Sturdee Avenue, Rosebank, Johannesburg 2196, South Africa

Penguin Books Ltd, Registered Offices:
80 Strand, London WC2R 0RL, England

First published in the United States of America by The Viking Press 1957
Published in Penguin Books 1977
This edition with an introduction by Robert Morsberger and Katharine Morsberger published 2007

THE LIBRARY OF CONGRESS HAS CATALOGED THE HARDCOVER EDITION AS FOLLOWS:
Steinbeck, John, 1902–1968.
The short reign of Pippin IV : a fabrication / John Steinbeck; introduction by Robert Morsberger and
Katharine Morsberger.
p. cm.—(Penguin classics)
Includes bibliographical references.
ISBN 978-0-14-303946-4
I. Morsberger, Robert Eustis, 1929– II. Morsberger, Katharine M. III. Title.
IV. Title: Short reign of Pippin the Fourth.
PS3537.T3234S5 2007
815'.52—dc22 2006052750

To my sister Esther

Contents

Introduction by Robert Morsberger and
   Katharine Morsberger   ix

Notes   xxix

Works Consulted   xxxiii

THE SHORT REIGN OF PIPPIN IV

Introduction

To his lifelong friend Webster F. Street, John Steinbeck wrote on March 20, 1956, ". . . without warning an idea happened that so charmed me that I couldn't shake it out. It is the wrong length, the wrong subject, and everything else is wrong with it except that it is fun and I could not resist writing it. I must say I do have fun with my profession, if that's what it is."[1] This irresistibly charming idea became *The Short Reign of Pippin IV,* the least known and least characteristic of Steinbeck's novels but the one he most enjoyed writing. Uncharacteristic because it is set in France rather than in California or Mexico, its characters are urban sophisticates rather than farmers, its dialogue has an urbane polish instead of being the talk of working men, and its droll humor is mostly gentle satire rather than the highjinks of *Tortilla Flat, Cannery Row,* and *Sweet Thursday.*

The idea that Steinbeck found so entertaining was to return the monarchy to France at a time when the Fourth Republic was so unstable that it was in danger of collapse. For the entire period of its existence, the Fourth Republic (1946–1958) was in decline; in its thirteen years, it had had a turnover of seventeen prime ministers and twenty-five cabinets.[2] Despite the fact that there have been royal pretenders and claimants to the throne of France ever since the French Revolution, the French government of the post–World War II years was still strongly republican; there was no real danger that it would replace democracy with royalty, though as recently as 1945, Michel Debré asserted that "the only chance for French democracy is, if the term may be used, a republican monarch."[3]

Steinbeck noted that "The Royalists of France, or for that

matter of any country where royalty has been eliminated as a
governing principle, have never given up."[4] What might happen, Steinbeck wondered, if a mild-mannered private citizen
who never conceived of being king, were picked from obscurity
and placed, against his will, upon the throne?

The subtitle of Steinbeck's *The Short Reign of Pippin IV* is
"A Fabrication," indicating that the reader is not to expect a
conventional novel but rather (according to the *Oxford English Dictionary*) "an invention," "a false statement," perhaps
a fantasy. "What is said to have happened might have been invented, and the occasion and motives for the fabrication may
be conceived."

Between 1952 and 1954, Steinbeck made three lengthy trips
to France, and this immersion in France doubtless influenced
his writing *The Short Reign of Pippin IV,* providing the occasions and some of the motives for this fabrication. In 1952,
after completing *East of Eden*, Steinbeck took his new wife,
Elaine Scott, to Europe for a second honeymoon. Elaine found
her husband to be an intense sightseer. Early in May, they went
to Paris, which Elaine had never seen before, and her husband,
who had been there briefly in 1946 and 1947, delighted in show-
ing her around.[5] To Pascal (Pat) Covici, his publisher and friend
at Viking, he wrote on May 12, "Paris is always wonderful—
both recognized and new every time."[6] Two weeks later, he
added, "Paris is so lovely. Elaine is already making plans to
come back before she has even gone away. Now and then we
get to disliking the French until we realize that they made this
country and no bad people could have done it."[7]

After exploring the city thoroughly, they bought a Citroën
and drove south through the French countryside to Geneva,[8]
stopping en route for five days in the wine country around
Poligny, where Steinbeck immersed himself in viniculture,[9] the
source of Pippin of Héristal's income. While in Geneva, Steinbeck wrote an article entitled "The Soul and Guts of France,"
which was published in *Colliers* (30 August 1952, pp. 26–28,
30). Then the Steinbecks proceeded over the Alps to Milan,
Venice, Florence, and Rome. In Venice, they were so popular
that Covici wrote them, "It wouldn't surprise me at all if you

were soon to be elected Duke, and Elaine Duchess, of Venice.[10] Could this have prompted the idea of returning the royalty to France? At any rate, Steinbeck joked to his agent, Elizabeth Otis, "I have decided to become a royalist. That is the only thing I have not been accused of. . . . Besides, royalists can and do remain in complete ignorance of any reality—a highly desirable state, I am beginning to believe."[11] The pieces for *Pippin IV* were beginning to fall into place. Another piece was motor scooters, which Steinbeck observed zipping all around Italy and on which he proposed writing an article for *Colliers*.[12] It did not materialize, but in his explorations incognito around Paris and its outskirts, Pippin putts around on a motor scooter.

By July, the Steinbecks were back in Paris, in time for Bastille Day on July 14, which they celebrated with a dinner at the Eiffel Tower restaurant with John Huston, José Ferrer, and some of the cast of *Moulin Rouge,* which Huston was then filming. They enjoyed the fireworks and afterward a sprawling street party.[13] On July 24, they proceeded to London, then to Ireland, and arrived home on August 31, barely in time for the publication of *East of Eden.*[14]

After a year and a half in the States, during which Steinbeck wrote *Sweet Thursday,* the Steinbecks returned to Europe in the spring of 1954, first to Portugal and Spain and then "following the spring," north to France and on to Scandinavia. In Paris, the Steinbecks stayed in a spectacular rental at Number One Avenue de Marigny, next door to the Rothschild mansion and across a courtyard from the President's palace. Steinbeck noted that it had been "the Paris headquarters of Knights of St. John,"[15] otherwise known as the Hospitallers, a noble order founded in the Middle Ages to provide charity and care for the infirm and poor. It was to become Pippin Héristal's home in the novel Steinbeck wrote two years later, where its origins would symbolize his idealism and concern for the well-being of his countrymen.

As always in France, Steinbeck was greeted with warmth and admiration. His French publishers hosted an enormous reception for the publication of *East of Eden,* at which he was surrounded by "at least five hundred influential people and twenty cameras and radio microphones."[16] As Graham Greene put it, "When you ask a Frenchman about American writers, they invariably put Steinbeck at the top of the list. He has exerted a strong pull on the French mind. And they do not discriminate between the early and the late Steinbeck—that's just a critical fetish that seems quite inadequate in this case. They like all of it."[17]

They liked it so much that the weekly *Figaro Littéraire* asked him to write a weekly article on Paris, which he enjoyed doing. In his opening contribution, Steinbeck stated, "I will offer you Paris, perhaps not as it is, but as I see it."[18] Delighted with his account of the city, the French Academy honored him with a formal dinner, and French writers, critics, and journalists came calling. Steinbeck was especially charmed when he was invited to serve at the writers' booth at the Kermesse aux Etoiles, an outdoor charity fair in the Tuileries, where hundreds of people lined up for him to sign *East of Eden,* the profits of which went to charity. When André Maurois advised him to slow down, Steinbeck began engaging the purchasers in conversation, learning about each individual.[19] The Steinbecks spent the fall wandering around Europe and were back in New York in time for Christmas.

The charm of Paris lingered with them, though in actuality, at the time before and during Steinbeck's writing *Pippin,* the French political scene was almost as chaotic as Steinbeck's fictional one. After its retreat from Dien Bien Phu in May 1954, France withdrew from a war in French Indochina against a nationalist-communist movement led by the Vietnamese Ho Chi Minh, a war that the United States subsequently renewed with tragic results. France granted independence to Morocco and Tunisia but became disastrously involved in a war against independence for Algeria. It was this war that finally brought down the Fourth Republic. When Steinbeck wrote *The Short Reign of Pippin IV,* the Fourth Republic had not yet fallen, but it was tottering.

In the United States, with the Cold War raging, McCarthyism exploited a dangerous paranoia to create a witch hunt against suspected Communists that Steinbeck called "a climate of fear and suspicion"[20] that crippled or ruined the careers and sometimes caused the suicides of people not only in the government but also in the arts. Steinbeck, who had been attacked himself as un-American for writing *The Grapes of Wrath*, was enraged. By the time Steinbeck was writing *Pippin IV*, Senator Joseph McCarthy was in disgrace as a liar, an unprincipled character assassin, and had been censured by the Senate. He died of alcoholism in 1957, the year that *The Short Reign of Pippin IV* was published. But that same year, the House Un-American Committee (H.U.A.C.), which was still in business, ordered Arthur Miller to testify, and when he refused, Miller was put on trial for contempt of Congress. Steinbeck was the only author who wrote on his behalf, publishing in *Esquire* a blistering attack on the witch-hunting of H.U.A.C.[21]

None of these political issues is referred to in *The Short Reign of Pippin IV*, which served Steinbeck as a sort of escape, but Steinbeck's disillusionment with the politics of the decade, which dominate his next and final novel, *The Winter of Our Discontent*, contribute to the cynicism that flows through *Pippin*. During the 1952 and 1956 presidential campaigns, Steinbeck was such an ardent supporter of Adlai Stevenson that he wrote speeches on his behalf, one of them read by Henry Fonda.[22] During the 1956 campaign, while he was writing *Pippin*, Steinbeck covered the national conventions for the *Louisville Courier-Journal* and about forty other papers[23] and the experience may have influenced his satire on the debates in the French National Assembly.

Though grim things were happening on both sides of the Atlantic, Steinbeck's satiric fable is generally genial and benevolent escapism. He does not mention the wars in Vietnam and Algeria but instead focuses on the wobbly nature of the French government after the end of World War II.

As the novel opens, the French government is in a state of chaos, splintered into a plethora of factions with cumbersome and conflicting titles, including literally dozens of political parties, with which Steinbeck has great fun coming up with such absurdities as the The Christian Atheists, The Christian Christians, The Christian Communists and three other kinds of Communists, the Conservative Radicals, and the Radical Conservatives. As the factions, headed by people with such ludicrous names as M. Rumorgue, M. Deuxcloches (Two Clocks), M. Douxpied (A Dozen Feet), struggle against each other, the only workable solution seems to be a return to the monarchy. After exhausting arguments in which every other option is eliminated, the members of the National Assembly decided to return to a branch of the monarchy sufficiently ancient and venerated that all can agree. These are the Merovingians, and their last legitimate descendant is Pippin Héristal, named for Pepin Héristal (680–714), the great-grandfather of Charlemagne. When informed of their choice, Pippin is horrified; he would much rather remain in obscurity, enjoying his collection of progressive jazz and practicing his hobby, astronomy, focused upon the heavens rather than on the earth. But when persuaded that France finds him indispensable to return stability and prosperity to the nation, he reluctantly consents.

The situation offered Steinbeck many opportunities for satire, comic and serious, both at the expense of France and of the United States. To Pascal Covici he wrote, "As for its excellence, I cannot give you an idea. . . . I'm pretty sure a lot of it is funny as hell and I think a lot of it is essentially true, but what its overall value is—I don't know. . . . I think I have said many things that must be said that should be said and that haven't been said. The spiritual father of this book is Candide and while I do not write as well as Voltaire I think I write much funnier."[24]

But Covici was not happy with Steinbeck's choice of a subject for his new novel. To his agent, Elizabeth Otis, Steinbeck wrote, "I am sure he doesn't like this kind of book but I'm pretty sure he was parroting Marshall [Best, managing editor at Viking] about how many copies it would sell. Hell, there is no surety that any of my books will sell and a lot of them haven't. . . . I know that he simply wants me to write the *Grapes of Wrath* over and over."[25] Actually, Covici proposed "a sequel to *The Pastures of Heaven*. I was to repeat it as of this generation. And that is a lovely idea except that the people who used to live in

the Valley don't anymore. New people moved in." Steinbeck
did not want to use "a vague memory of Monterey County of
my childhood."[26] It was no longer his country.

Covici remained unenthusiastic about Steinbeck's satire on
the return of royalty to France and objected that its historical
background was too obscure for American readers. In response, Steinbeck wrote, "I do not and will not agree with Pat
that the historical date [data] must come out because someone
may not understand it. If the reader doesn't know what a
Merovingian is, let him find out or buy some other book."[27]
Since the reader has already bought this book, a brief account
of the Merovingians is in order.

As the Dark Ages began to evolve into the Middle Ages, the
Merovingian dynasty of shadowy, forgotten kings (who claimed
a descent from mythological deities) with names like Chlodomire,
Childéric, Childibert, Chlotar, the spectacularly evil Chilperic,
Guntramn, and Dagobert, which for several centuries had ruled
the Franks and Gaul in parts of what were to become France,
faded away and was replaced by the Carolingian dynasty.

Prominent in the twilight of the Merovingians was a series of
rulers named Pepin (which Steinbeck anglicized to Pippin),
who began to unify the Franks. Pepin I was not actually a king
but was a great landlord who controlled the royal finances,
commanded the army, and held the title "mayor of the palace"
during the time of *les rois fainéants* (the idle or do-nothing
kings), who lived in reclusive debauchery, leaving the mayors
of the palace to run the government. Pepin's grandson Pepin II
of Héristal (680–714), who spoke both French and German,
further unified the Franks. When the Moors, having conquered
Spain, tried to extend their conquest into Gaul, the illegitimate
son of Pepin II, Charles, defeated them in a decisive battle at
Tours in 732, drove them back over the Pyrenees, and permanently stopped their advance into France. For this victory, he
earned the surname Carolus Martellus or Charles Martel (the
Hammer).

Charles's son Pepin inherited the title of mayor of the palace
but asked Pope Zachariah whether he could without sin depose
the listless *roi fainéant* and make himself the actual king. The

pope responded that the person who really wielded the power was more deserving of the crown than the idle king who did not. With this encouragement, in 751, Pepin called an assembly of nobles and bishops at Poisson, where they deposed Childeric III and unanimously elected Pepin king. "To us," declared Pepin III, "the Lord hath entrusted the care of government."[28] In turn Pepin campaigned beyond the Alps on behalf of the Pope, to whom he gave some of his conquest, extending the Papal State with the Donation of Pepin. In 754, Pope Stephen II journeyed to St. Denis, where he anointed Pepin *rex Dei gratia,* "king by the grace of God." Known as Pepin "the Short," Pepin III further unified the Franks and helped create a rise in Frankish culture until his death in 768. He was the most effectual, epoch-making king before his son Charles, who earned the name Charles the Great, Carolus Magnus, or Charlemagne, and ushered in the Carolingian dynasty. Will Durant sums up Pepin as "a patient and far-seeing ruler, pious and practical, loving peace and invincible in war, and moral beyond any royal precedent in the Gaul of those centuries. All that Charlemagne accomplished was prepared by Pepin. . . ."[29]

Though Covici was unhappy with Steinbeck's work in progress, the author was enjoying himself immensely. His wife stated that, "I can't remember when John seemed to be having so much fun with a book"[30] and that she could hear him "chuckling and laughing while he wrote."[31] For him, it was a *jeu d'esprit.* Steinbeck himself called it "surely a self-indulgence," though he added that "it is more than just a clever idea. . . . I find that I almost completely believe in it."[32]

Having decided to write a satire about the restoration of the monarchy in France, Steinbeck next questioned what sort of things to satirize. One that offered lots of harmlessly amusing possibilities was the anachronistic trappings of royalty. While he was a grim realist in his proletarian fiction, as a lifelong admirer of Sir Thomas Malory's *Le Morte D'Arthur,* Steinbeck was also a romantic who collected swords, daggers, bows, and spears and spent most of a summer teaching his son Thom how to construct medieval weapons, including a catapult. Steinbeck liked ceremonial costumes and told Elaine, "I have the soul to wear a cape and plumes and carry a sword, but I have the physique to be always handed a hod."[33] In the 1950s, he liked to go to town wearing an opera cape and flourishing a broad swash-buckler's hat. When he became a member of the American Acad-emy of Arts and Letters, he asked the Academy to send him "any regalia, buttons, ribbons, small swords, etc., as are befitting to my academic grandeur," and when he learned there were none except buttons, he expressed himself "disappointed at the lack of regalia. The French Academy meets dressed in cocked hats, embroidered vests, and small swords."[34]

For his wife's birthday while they were in Paris in the summer of 1954, Steinbeck borrowed a large chateau on the outskirts of Paris that had belonged to Louis IV's finance minister. As Stein-beck's friends the Bucks recalled, the arriving guests found every window of the chateau lit by candles and were met by Stein-beck's sons carrying torches and dressed in livery, who escorted them into the candelabra-lit ballroom. "Truly," said Joyce Buck, "you felt you were back in the eighteenth century."[35]

Weapons and armor figure in *Pippin IV* mostly for spectacle, as do costumes from the medieval world to the *ancien regime* just before the Revolution. Carriage makers and armorers have a field day as their skills become once more in demand. Great Britain, one of the countries that still retains a monarchy, has coaches, fanfare, pomp and circumstance, Victorian-costumed guards at Buckingham Palace, sixteenth-century-costumed "beefeaters" at the Tower of London, and bewigged barristers, all of which are good for the tourist trade in an era where roy-alty is primarily ceremonial rather than political.

In *Pippin IV,* except when the delegates to the National As-sembly regress to the code of dueling during the debate over the choice of a monarch and "Hardly a gentleman there was who did not wear scratches and cuts which proclaimed that his honor was intact,"[36] all this regression to or re-creation of the past is harmless enough, like the Society for Creative Anachronism.

All of these anachronisms are colorful and dramatic, but they become comic when Steinbeck blends them in a sort of historical potpourri. During Pippin's coronation, the proces-sion includes modern tanks and weapons, heavy tractor-drawn artillery, together with crossbowmen in medieval attire, "dragoons with burnished breastplates," a "Noble Youth in full armor," and paratroopers carrying submachine guns, followed by seventeenth-century "musketeers in lace, knee-breeches, silk stockings, and high-heeled shoes with great buckles."[37] Miss France collapses with a crash from the weight and heat of wearing armor like Joan of Arc.

One of the more entertaining anachronisms in the return of royalty was the custom for monarchs to have one or more mistresses. Most notable in France were such pairs as Charles VII and Agnes Sorel, Henri II and Diane de Poitiers, Louis XIV and Louise de la Vallière and the Marquise de Montespan, Louis XV and Madame de Pompadour and Madame du Barry. Even in modern times, presidents and prime ministers have had mistresses officially recognized with pensions and prominent positions at their lover's funeral. Consequently, though Pippin Héristal is monogamous, he is required to have a mistress as one of the trappings of royalty. The situation is ludicrous; the Folies Bergère hold a competition to choose the King's Mistress. The one that is selected for him is a proper lady whom he never even meets and whose name he does not know. But royal protocal requires him to have her, and even his wife agrees.

Another anachronism is that the king must reside in the royal palace of Versailles. Versailles may seem a vast improvement over the shacks and bunkhouses provided for Steinbeck's migrant workers of the 1930s and from the Palace Flophouse of Cannery Row. But though it is an impressive tourist trap, Versailles has not been kept up since the French Revolution, unlike Windsor Castle and Buckingham Palace, which the British have fitted out with the most modern comforts. Consequently, Pippin finds that Versailles is about as uncomfortable as the Middle Ages was for Mark Twain's Connecticut Yankee. "It's drafty there," he complains to his Uncle Charlie. "The beds are horrible. The floors creak." It is so cold that the two hundred soi-disant aristocrats who consider themselves entitled to move in with the king are smashing up the furniture for firewood. The queen is disgusted by their posturing, bowing, and scrap-

ing, and expecting her to provide their meals, while Pippin calls
these hangers-on bums. Housekeeping is a nightmare for the
queen, who considers the palace a "gigantic old dustbox" with
antiquated plumbing and seventeenth-century kitchens impos-
sibly far away from the royal apartments. The ladies-in-waiting
refuse to demean themselves by doing anything useful.

Pippin's wife, Marie, is an unimaginative, bored, and sometimes nagging housewife who admires but does not understand
her scholarly husband. She is overwhelmed by having to run
the household at Versailles. Their daughter, Clotilde, however,
is a hilarious example of the liberated woman, another target
of Steinbeck's genial satire.

Despite the fact that French women had long been distinguished in the arts and sciences, it was not until the end of
World War II that they started to become liberated. Not unil
1944 were they given the right to vote, perhaps in recognition
of their work in the Resistance,[38] and soon women were elected
as deputies to the Constituent Assemblies and afterward, the
National Assembly, though their numbers in the Assembly
dwindled in the 1950s. Domestically, their standard of living
improved with many labor-saving devices, and the appearance
of *Elle* magazine and Christian Dior and Coco Chanel designer
clothes appealed to women who wanted to become more chic
and alluring. But a law passed in 1920 and still in effect in
the 1950s outlawed contraception and criminalized abortion.[39]
Simone de Beauvoir's book *The Second Sex* (1949) fought
against the lingering inequality of women, and by the time the
Steinbecks were visiting France, some Frenchwomen were acting very liberated indeed.

Some of Steinbeck's satire deals with the uninhibited antics
of Pippin's precocious daughter, Clotilde (her name is taken from
a Merovingian queen), who at age fifteen published a novel,
Adieu Ma Vie, in revolt "against everything she could think of,"
which was made into a movie. Then at sixteen, she became
prominent in politics as a Communist but considered dropping
out and becoming a nun dedicated to giving pedicures to the
poor. Instead, she engendered a cult of Clotdisme, a philosophy

of fashionable despair that inspired "sixty-eight adolescents to commit suicide by leaping from the top of the Arc de Triomphe." She fought several rapier duels with Academicians and gave wretched performances in several epic movies before becoming a princess. It would seem that some of her notoriety would have attached itself to her father, but when Pippin is proposed to be the monarch of France, no one objects to his daughter, whose activities were condemned by the church, or even mentions her. Pippin himself seems to respond to her erratic careers with mild amusement.

Clotilde is based, with considerable exaggeration, upon Françoise Sagan (the pseudonym of François Quirex, 1935–). With the publication when she was eighteen of her first novel, *Bonjour Tristesse* (1954), a best-selling picture of disillusioned and embittered French sophisticates, Sagan became an international celebrity with the very sort of people she was writing about. Her second novel, *Un Certain Sourire* came out in 1956, the year before *The Short Reign of Pippin IV*. A film of *Bonjour Tristesse* was released in 1958; it features a moody and precocious teenager who breaks up an affair her widowed playboy father is enjoying by destroying his mistress on the French Riviera. *Un Certain Sourire* (also released as a film in 1958) concerns a romance between a young Parisian couple studying at the Sorbonne that is broken off when the young woman is seduced by a rich, older, married *roué*. Both leave a bitter taste of disillusionment.

After an interesting, eccentric beginning as a prodigy, Clotilde falls in love with a visiting American, Tod Johnson, whose multimillionaire father is the Egg King of Petaluma, California, and she spends the rest of the novel languishing over him.

Pippin Héristal is a reluctant king. He loves his former placid life, his astronomical hobby, his basically being left alone. He wants no part of the trappings of royalty nor the duties of office. As Shakespeare put it, "Uneasy lies the head that wears the crown." But once Pippin agrees to accept that crown, he determines to govern as well as he can. For practical advice, he consults his uncle Charles Martel, a dealer in art and antiques, named for the victor of the battle of Tours. But Uncle Charlie is a consummate con man, who passes off fake paintings as unsigned

works by Renoir, Boucher, Roualt, and other masters and justi-
fies his swindles by saying that "A man must live." He addresses
Pippin like a priest giving absolution to a penitent, calling him
"my son," "my child," but his advice is invariably cynical, trying
to dissuade Pippin from his impractical ideals. Uncle Charlie in-
troduces Pippin to Tod Johnson, and the two of them introduce
him to martinis, to which he is becoming addicted.

Through Tod Johnson, Steinbeck funnels his satire on the
United States. Tod's father is a self-made man who hates liber-
alism and Democrats. Tod is far more open-minded and con-
fesses to Pippin that his father would be horrified to know that
he voted Democratic in the last presidential election. But
although Steinbeck calls Tod "the ideal American young man,"
who is enamored of Pippin's daughter and shares Pippin's
enthusiasm for progressive jazz, Tod is also skeptical of the
king's idealism and shares Uncle Charlie's materialism, learning
his business, planning to open fraudulent art galleries in major
American cities, and proposing that the two of them team up to
sell French titles to American millionaires. When Pippin protests
that such trickery is not right, Tod replies, "What do you mean
by right?"[40] He believes that the main questions in business are
"What have you got to sell and who is going to buy and have
they got the money?"[41] Never mind business ethics. Tod's philosophy is "The first function of business is to create the demand and the second to fulfill it." When Pippin argues that, "It
seems to me reprehensible to search out areas of weakness and
to exploit them," Tod asks, "Aren't you going to have some difficulty being king, sir?" He adds that as king, "You've got a
great little thing here, great, but it can blow up in your face if
you don't play your cards right."[42]

At Pippin's request, Tod gives him lessons in American democracy, but Tod may not be a reliable advisor. He tells Pippin that
it doesn't make much difference which major party is in power.
Steinbeck, a staunchly liberal Democrat, would not agree. Tod's
most provocative analysis is that the real government consists
of corporations, who rule benevolently, claiming to hate socialism yet providing pensions, medical care, accident insurance,
vacations, and most of the benefits of the welfare state, not out

of kindness but out of pragmatism, figuring that healthy, happy workers will be more productive and be able to buy their products. To some extent this was true in the 1950s, when the American Dream of middle-class prosperity was probably closer than it ever was before, half a century before it turned into the growing nightmare of twenty-first-century cutthroat corporate greed and corruption. Nevertheless, Tod is an apostle of crass materialism who sees nothing wrong with rigging tax laws. Despite their friendship, Tod and Pippin are antagonists, Tod wanting to look out for number one, while Pippin wants whatever is best for the people as a whole.

Seeking solace, Pippin goes to a third confidante, his wife's old school friend Suzanne Lescault, who worked as a nude dancer at the Folies Bergère until her arches fell, after which she became a nun, Sister Hyacinthe, who offers Pippin kindly, benevolent advice, mixed with platonic flirtation. She provides comfort but little else.

During Pippin's brief reign, France prospers, as foreign loans and investments pour in, tourism thrives, and nature provides idyllic weather that promises a bountiful harvest. But Pippin himself accomplishes little and spends most of his time preparing himself to lead France. Brushing up on French history, Pippin identifies with Louis XVI, who would rather have been a clock maker than king (just as Pippin would rather remain an astronomer), who was the best of the Bourbons but was guillotined for crimes of his ancestors rather than for his own. Pippin says, "To a certain extent I think I am like him. I am trying to see where he made his errors. I should hate to fall into the same trap."[43]

Having led a sheltered life, Pippin sneaks out of the palace incognito whenever he can, like the *Arabian Nights* Caliph Haroun-al Raschid and the medieval French Louis XI, and goes around Paris and its environs to see what France is really like, not only getting to know the ordinary people, whom Steinbeck called "the soul and guts of France"[44] but also inspecting the infrastructure and examining wages, prices, the cost and condition of rented buildings, and the operations of the market. Ironically, his various disguises look ridiculous and give him away, and he finds that his own bland appearance allows him to be overlooked and escape from his bodyguards better than wigs, false moustaches, and other theatrical getup. To go a bit farther afield, he takes to driving a motor scooter.

When Uncle Charlie warns that his idealism, if put into practice, may bring retaliation against him, perhaps even a tumbril to a guillotine, Pippin's reply is scathing. "I did not ask to be king . . . but I am king and I find this dear, rich, productive France torn by selfish factions, fleeced by greedy promoters, deceived by parties. I find that there are six hundred ways of avoiding taxes if you are rich enough—sixty-five methods of raising rent in controlled rental areas. The riches of France, which should have some kind of distribution, are gobbled up. . . . And on this favored land the maggots are feeding."[45] Though Pippin speaks about France, Steinbeck made similar charges about conditions in the United States, and his anger would come to a head in his next and final novel, *The Winter of Our Discontent,* which tipped the scales of the judges to award him the Nobel Prize.

The nature of leadership has been an ongoing concern throughout Steinbeck's fiction, from his first novel, *Cup of Gold,* about the seventeenth-century pirate Henry Morgan, who became knighted and made governor of Jamaica. It resurfaces prominently in *In Dubious Battle,* in which, on the one hand, an unscrupulous veteran Communist organizer instructs a novice in how to organize a strike and manipulate the workers, not for their own benefit (he wants some of them to be killed) but for the ultimate aims of the party, and on the other hand, Doc Burton, who believes in benevolent cooperation. A key scene in *The Grapes of Wrath* occurs when the indomitable Ma Joad takes over the leadership of the family from the dispirited Pa. In "The Leader of the People," Grandfather's richest memory is of having led a wagon train across the West. In *The Moon Is Down,* there are two kinds of leadership. In opposition to the Nazi "herd men" who conquer Norway, the townspeople also act as a group, unregimented but spontaneously cooperating in resistance to terrorize and sabotage the invaders. Except for the Quisling, Corell, the free citizens act as one man. Corell's

response is to advise the Nazis, "When we have killed the leaders, the rebellion will be broken."[46] The issue of leadership thus
focuses not on the Fuehrer but on Mayor Orden, who insists
that his people "don't like to have others think for them," that
"authority is in the town" and not in any individual, and that
he simply carries out the collective will of the community.[47]

The genuine leader for Steinbeck is not one who seeks or seizes
power but one who represents the community. This is the sort
of leadership that Emiliano Zapata acquires in Steinbeck's
screenplay *Viva Zapata!* in which Zapata tells the campesinos
shortly before his death, "About leaders. You've looked for
leaders. For strong men without faults. There aren't any. There
are only men like yourselves. . . . There's no leader but yourselves." Like Pippin, Zapata has not sought leadership and re-
sists having it thrust upon him, but he cannot resist taking
action when he encounters episodes of cruelty and oppression
and thus, against his will, becomes a leader of the Mexican revolution. When he resigns from high office, rather than become
dictatorial, he is betrayed and assassinated. Leadership of various sorts is also an issue in Steinbeck's screenplay *Lifeboat*,
Cannery Row, and *The Wayward Bus*.

The Steinbeck novel immediately preceding *The Short Reign
of Pippin IV* is *Sweet Thursday*, a comparatively short and
lightweight sequel to *Cannery Row*. Among the boisterous
bums who pal around with Doc is a lovable simpleton named
Hazel, who is dumbfounded when Fauna, the new madam of
the Bear Flag brothel, reads his horoscope and proclaims that
he will become president of the United States. He no more
wants to be president than Pippin Héristal wants to be king. "If
there had been any avenue of escape he would have taken it but
his horoscope closed all doors."[48] Pippin, a well-educated man
and amateur scientist, in addition to having royal lineage, is
well qualified to be king, despite his reluctance, but Hazel is an
ignorant lunkhead, who nevertheless takes the horoscope seriously, and being condemned to accept his duty and his fate, is
sick with anxiety and loneliness. "The dignity of his position
was greater than himself. He could not let his future down."[49]

The entire situation is ridiculous, but Hazel rises to the occasion, which he thinks requires him to break one of Doc's arms in order to end the estrangement between Doc and the woman he loves. Despite his success as a matchmaker, Hazel pleads to be freed from the doom of becoming president, so Fauna lets him off the hook by telling him she made a mistake in reading his horoscope. Though this narrative is ludicrous, it has a sort of lopsided logic and may have pointed Steinbeck in the direction of Pippin Héristal's reluctant reign as king of France.

Pippin's reign comes to its end when, after months of thoughtful preparation, he presides over a new constitutional convention and presents his "Code Pippin." It is benevolent, idealistic, humanitarian, befitting the "sense of mission, of divinity of purpose"[50] that he has said he needs. Denouncing the greedy oligarchy of wealth that he says is destroying the nation, he proposes to bring back a more equitable distribution of wealth by lowering taxes and closing loopholes, by raising wages, controlling prices, streamlining government, strengthening pensions and public health insurance, and breaking up great land holdings. He proposes adding "Opportunity" to the motto "Liberty, Equality, Fraternity." When both the Right and Left are dumbfounded, he speaks out in cold anger, telling them, "I didn't ask to be king. . . . I begged not to be king. And you didn't want a king. You wanted a patsy. . . . But you elected a king, and by God you've got a king—or a gigantic joke."[51]

Unfortunately, Steinbeck settles for the gigantic joke. Implausibly, the king is dressed in a marshal's uniform rented from a theatrical costumer that is grotesquely too large, the sagging, baggy pants held up with safety pins, which rip apart as he leaves the stage, exposing him to ridicule and howls of laughter. The king's finest hour ends in a pratfall. And his mildly liberal proposal so outrages the vested interests of Right and Left that they incite a riot, and Sister Hyacinthe urges the king to flee for his life. But while he is disappointed in France's reversion to its turbulent chaos, he does not believe the people are so far gone that they will resurrect the Reign of Terror. Instead of fleeing across the border, he goes home, like Candide, to cultivate his own garden. As for France, the Fourth Republic did collapse a year later, and was replaced by a Fifth Republic, to be headed not by a descendant of Charlemagne, but by another "grand Charles," Charles De Gaulle.

As the publication date for *Pippin* approached, Viking became increasingly apprehensive. Steinbeck wrote to Elizabeth Otis, "There's a great unease about it at Viking, but there's an unease all over and maybe one thing transmits to another."[52] According to Steinbeck's biographer, Jackson Benson, "Marshall Best recalls that there were seven different readings of the manuscript and that it was the only book that Viking tried to persuade John not to publish. In large part because there was so much opposition to it—both Elizabeth and Pat had come to hate it—the book took a place close to his heart."[53] Apparently, Viking feared that a book so different from what readers had come to expect from Steinbeck would drive them away, and that a lightweight comedy from the author of *The Grapes of Wrath* would further damage his reputation that the anti-Steinbeck claque of the literary establishment, like Maxwell Geismar, had been attacking.

But though it is often hilarious, Steinbeck's satiric novel has serious undertones; and while he admitted that he wrote it almost entirely for his own amusement, he insisted, "It is more than just a clever idea I believe and should be given that dignity. . . . I find that I almost completely believe in it. . . . It certainly shows very little mercy to anyone. As a matter of fact I rather think the French will like it. It is the Americans who won't, but the Americans I am afraid have very little humor. This damn thing has almost a Kafka overtone but it is written as history which indeed it is."[54] To Viking's surprise and delight, when *Pippin* was published in the spring of 1957, it was picked as a Main Selection by the Book-of-the-Month Club with an enthusiastic report by Basil Davenport in the *Book-of-the-Month Club News*. Calling the oft-told story of a commoner turned temporarily into a king "one of the universal fantasies," Davenport agrees with Steinbeck that along with the book's "high-spirited foolery," in the "discussions about the nature of government the reader will decidedly find something to think about. . . . This is that rare find, a book of humor that is also a book of ideas." Readers apparently thought so too, for despite Viking's fears, it sold extremely well. Steinbeck asked Covici to send copies of *Pippin* to Harry Truman, Adlai Stevenson, and Moss Hart (because he thought the book might be staged or screened).[55] American critics gave *Pippin* mixed reviews. Elizabeth Janeway, in *The New York Times,* advised readers not to take it too seriously and to "enjoy the fabrication," while B. R. Redman in the *Saturday Review* complained that it was "thin broth." Daniel George in *Spectator* called it "delightful," while *Time* responded with a yawn. *The Library Journal* found it "highly enjoyable"; H. T. Moore in *The New Republic* found it "superficially amusing." William Hogan in *The New Yorker* called it "a very pleasant Steinbeckian surprise."

Some academic critics enjoyed Steinbeck's *jeu d'esprit,* which Warren French considered "the most entertaining novel that Steinbeck had written since *Cannery Row.*"[56] Others saw *Pippin* as a further sign of what they considered the author's decline. To Elizabeth Otis, Steinbeck responded that the reviews "follow exactly the old pattern I am so used to, celebrating old books which the same people raised hell with when they were printed."[57] Even some scholars specializing in Steinbeck treated *Pippin* with contempt. Peter Lisca, whose *The Wide World of John Steinbeck,* published just a year after *Pippin IV,* is one of the first major book-length studies of Steinbeck, helped set the tone of criticism that finds a continuing decline in Steinbeck's postwar work, a judgment that has subsequently been challenged successfully by John Disky, Louis Owens, and others. Lisca damned the novel not for what it was but for what it was not, claiming it lacked the substance and style of the early Steinbeck books.[58] Joseph Fontenrose called it "tasteless" and Richard Astro termed it "sapless and languid." Lester J. Marks faulted the book for not continuing the thematic designs of Steinbeck's earlier novels.[59] But as one of Steinbeck's friends maintained, "John was not an institution with institutional responsibilities—why shouldn't he do what he wanted to do?"[60]

John Ditsky, who worked on rehabilitating the novels of the 1950s from critical disdain, examining Steinbeck's later works on their own terms and appreciating the author's ability to change, rather than faulting them for not being like his earlier works, argues that "Pippin is due for an overview of the critical attitudes it has inspired to date, and equally as much for some sort of new statement of its lasting significance."[61]

In the British Isles, reviews were almost entirely enthusiastic. The *Illustrated London News* called it "very funny and agreeable." The *Sheffield Telegraph* found the novel "delicately worked out" and concluded that "the reader is rewarded by a brilliant exercise in satire." The *Tablet* termed it "an altogether successful political joke about France today that is at once gay, lighthearted, and immensely shrewd . . . I can only recommend it as the best lighthearted novel I have come across in years." The *Daily Telegraph* found "wisdom as well as wit in this Voltairean squib." The *Irish Press* called *Pippin* "pure Steinbeck, as gentle and human and joyous as *Cannery Row.*" Wolf Mankowitz, writing in the *Tribune* that the novel was "great fun," was glad to find that Steinbeck "has not lost that gift for indignation at social injustice which has made much of his work distinguished." The *New Statesman* called it "both an engaging and a sensible jape, fun to read, and with all the exhilaration of a sober writer's holiday-piece." The *Bookman* concluded that "if ever there was a book worth reading twice, this is it."

In France, when the novel was serialized in *Figaro* prior to its hardcover publication, it received glowing reviews. When the Steinbecks returned to France in June 1957, Steinbeck's French publisher celebrated the novel with a party on the Seine, aboard a bateau done up as a royal barge and flying the banner of Charlemagne.[62]

The last word belongs to Steinbeck, who wrote to Pascal Covici after the novel's publication that

> . . . anyone who in our humorless times who has concealed a sense of play, can, I believe, get an illegal chuckle from this book. In our scowling era, laughter may well be the only counter-revolutionary weapon.

I can imagine that future critics, if any survive, may view our ridiculous antics with hilarious laughter. And to that desirable end, *The Short Reign of Pippin IV* is dedicated.

Yours conspiratorially,
John[63]

NOTES

1. Elaine Steinbeck and Robert Wallsten, eds., *Steinbeck, A Life in Letters* (New York: Viking, 1975), p. 524.
2. Simon Serfaty, *France, De Gaulle, and Europe* (Baltimore: The Johns Hopkins Press, 1968), p. xii.
3. Robert Gildea, *France Since 1945* (New York and Oxford: Oxford University Press, 1996), p. 32.
4. John Steinbeck, *The Short Reign of Pippin IV* (New York: Viking, 1957; Penguin, 2007), p. 40.
5. Jackson J. Benson, *The True Adventures of John Steinbeck, Writer* (New York: Viking, 1984), p. 709; Jay Parini, *John Steinbeck, A Biography* (New York: Henry Holt, 1995), p. 355–356.
6. Thomas Fensch, *Steinbeck and Covici: The Story of a Friendship* (Middlebury, Vermont: Paul S. Eriksson, 1979), p. 178.
7. Ibid., p. 185.
8. Parini, p. 357.
9. Benson, pp. 712–713.
10. Ibid., p. 714.
11. Ibid, p. 749.
12. Ibid., pp. 714–715.
13. Ibid., p. 725; Parini, p. 359.
14. Parini, p. 360.
15. *Pippin*, p. 12.
16. Benson, p. 750.
17. Parini, p. 375.
18. Ibid., Benson, p. 752.
19. Benson, pp. 755–756.
20. Ibid., p. 759.
21. John Steinbeck, "The Trial of Arthur Miller," *Esquire*, June, 1957, 86.
22. Benson, p. 735.
23. Ibid., pp. 793–794.

24. Fensch, p. 196.
25. Benson, p. 474.
26. Ibid., p. 795.
27. Ibid., p. 794.
28. C. W. Previté, *The Shorter Cambridge Medieval History* (Cambridge: Cambridge University Press, 1952), vol. 1, p. 297.
29. Will Durant, *The Age of Faith* (New York: Simon & Schuster, 1950), p. 461. In 2003, the Merovingian monarchy reappeared in fiction in Dan Brown's phenomenally popular novel *The Da Vinci Code*. Leading its readers through a labyrinth of codes within codes within codes leading to other codes, Brown argues with considerable ingenuity but nothing that would weigh as evidence that Jesus Christ was wholly human, not divine, that he married Mary Magdalene, and intended her rather than St. Peter to be the head of the church, that male and female symbolism make her rather than a chalice, into the Holy Grail, that her womb is the Sangreal (sang real = royal blood), a symbol of the life-bringing "lost goddess" of antiquity. But, Brown argues, a conspiracy of misogynistic churchmen have plotted for two milennia to cover this up, "that almost everything our fathers taught us about Christ is false" (Dan Brown, *The Da Vinci Code* (New York: Doubleday, 2003), p. 235), that *The New Testament* is basically a lie. Brown goes on to claim that Jesus and Mary Magdalene had a child named Sarah, that Mary and Sarah escaped to France, and that the royal bloodline of Jesus and Mary Magdalene became the Merovingian kings of France. By this token, Pippin IV and his daughter Clotilde would be descendents of Jesus Christ and Mary Magdalene. Brown gets so carried away with his thesis that he finds supporting symbolism everywhere, even arguing that the heroine's red hair in the Walt Disney movie *The Little Mermaid* is a symbol of Mary Magdalene (Brown, p. 262). Historically, all this is hokum, and Steinbeck would probably have some scathingly ironic comments on it.
30. Parini, p. 390.
31. Benson, p. 785.
32. Ibid.
33. Ibid., pp. 808–809.
34. Ibid., p. 756.
35. Ibid., p. 764.
36. *Pippin*, p. 42.
37. Ibid., p. 74.
38. Gildea, p. 119.

39. Ibid., p. 121.
40. *Pippin*, p. 122.
41. Ibid., p. 121.
42. Ibid., p. 101, 105.
43. Ibid., p. 67.
44. John Steinbeck, "The Soul and Guts of France," *Colliers* 30 (August 30, 1952), pp. 26–28.
45. *Pippin*, pp. 137–138.
46. John Steinbeck, *The Moon Is Down* (New York: Viking, 1942), p. 171.
47. Ibid., p. 36, 41.
48. John Steinbeck, *Sweet Thursday* (New York: Viking, 1954), p. 212.
49. Ibid., p. 213.
50. *Pippin*, p. 97.
51. Ibid., p. 174.
52. *Life in Letters,* p. 541.
53. Benson, p. 803.
54. Ibid., pp. 785–786.
55. Fensch, p. 199.
56. Donald V. Coers, Paul D. Ruffin, Robert J. DeMott, eds., *After The Grapes of Wrath: Essays on John Steinbeck in Honor of Tetsumaro Hayashi* (Athens: Ohio University Press, 1995), p. 16.
57. Parini, p. 399.
58. Peter Lisca, *The Wide World of John Steinbeck* (New Brunswick, New Jersey: Rutgers University Press, 1958), pp. 263–264.
59. Joseph Fontenrose, *John Steinveck: An Introduction and Interpretation* (New York, Holt, Rinehart and Winston, 1963), p. 130; Richard Astro, *John Steinbeck and Edward F. Ricketts: The Shaping of a Novelist* (Minneapolis: University of Minnesota Press, 1973), p. 213; Lester J. Marks, *Thematic Design in the Novels of John Steinbeck* (The Hague: Mouton, 1969), p. 133.
60. Benson, p. 706.
61. John Ditsky, " 'Some Sense of Mission': Steinbeck's *The Short Reign of Pippin IV* Reconsidered," *Steinbeck Quarterly* 16 (1983), p. 79.
62. Benson, p. 815.
63. *A Life in Letters,* p. 538.

Works Consulted

Astro, Richard. *John Steinbeck and Edward F. Ricketts: The Shaping of a Novelist.* Minneapolis: University of Minnesota Press, 1973.

Benson, Jackson J. *The True Adventures of John Steinbeck, Writer.* New York: Viking, 1984.

Brown, Dan. *The Da Vinci Code.* New York: Doubleday, 2003.

Coers, Donald V., Paul D. Ruffin, and Robert J. DeMott, eds. *After* The Grapes of Wrath: *Essays on John Steinbeck in Honor of Tetsumaro Hayashi.* Athens, Ohio: Ohio University Press, 1995.

Ditsky, John. "'Some Sense of Mission': Steinbeck's *The Short Reign of Pippin IV* Reconsidered." *Steinbeck Quarterly* 16 (1983), 79–89.

Fensch, Thomas. *Steinbeck and Covici: The Story of a Friendship.* Middlebury, Vermont: Paul S. Eriksson, 1979.

Fontenrose, Joseph. *John Steinbeck: An Introduction and Interpretation.* New York: Holt, Rinehart and Winston, 1963.

French, Warren. *John Steinbeck,* 2nd ed. Boston: G. K. Hall, 1975.

Gildea, Robert. *France Since 1945.* New York: Oxford University Press, 1996.

Lisca, Peter. *The Wide World of John Steinbeck.* New Brunswick, N.J.: Rutgers University Press, 1958.

McMillan, James F. *Dreyfus to de Gaulle: Politics and Society in France 1898–1969.* London: Edward Arnold, 1985.

McMillan, James, ed. *Modern France 1880–2002.* New York: Oxford University Press, 2003.

Owens, Louis. "Steinbeck's 'Deep Dissembler': *The Short Reign of Pippin IV,*" *The Short Novels of John Steinbeck*, ed. Jackson J. Benson. Durham, N.C.: Duke University Press, 1990.

Parini, Jay. *John Steinbeck, A Biography.* New York: Henry Holt and Company, 1995.

Park, Julian, ed. *The Culture of France in Our Time.* Ithaca, N.Y.: Cornell University Press, 1954.

Rucklin, Christine. "Beyond France: Steinbeck's *The Short Reign of Pippin IV.*" In *Beyond Boundaries: Rereading John Steinbeck,* ed. Susan Shillinglaw and Kevin Hearle.

Serfaty, Simon. *France, De Gaulle, and Europe: The Policy of the Fourth and Fifth Republics Toward the Continent.* Baltimore: The Johns Hopkins Press, 1968.

Singer, Barnett. *Modern France: Mind, Politics, Society.* Seattle and London: University of Washington Press, 1980.

Steinbeck, Elaine and Robert Wallsten, eds. *Steinbeck, A Life in Letters.* New York: Viking, 1975.

Steinbeck, John. "The Soul and Guts of France." *Colliers* 30 (August 30, 1952), 26–28, 30.

Watt, F. W. *John Steinbeck*. New York: Grove Press, 1962.

Williams, Philip M. *Wars, Plots and Scandals in Post-War France.* Cambridge: Cambridge University Press, 1970.

The Short Reign
of Pippin IV

Number One Avenue de Marigny in Paris is a large, square house of dark and venerable appearance. The mansion is on the corner where de Marigny crosses the Avenue Gabriel, a short block from the Champs Elysées and across the street from the Elysée Palace, which is the home of the president of France. Number One abuts on a glass-roofed courtyard, on the other side of which is a tall and narrow building, once the stables and coachmen's quarters. On the ground level are still the stables, very elegant with carved marble mangers and water troughs, but upstairs there are three pleasant floors, a small but pleasant house in the center of Paris. On the second floor large glass

doors open on the unglassed portion of the courtyard which
connects the two buildings.

It is said that Number One, together with its coach house,
was built as the Paris headquarters of the Knights of St. John,
but it is presently owned and occupied by a noble French family who for a number of years have leased the converted coach
house, the use of the courtyard, and half of the flat connecting
roof to M. Pippin Arnulf Héristal and his family, consisting of
his wife, Marie, and his daughter, Clotilde. Soon after leasing
the stable house, M. Héristal called on his noble landlord and
requested permission to set up the base and mount for an eight-
inch refracting telescope on the portion of the flat roof to
which he had access. This request was granted, and thereafter,
since M. Héristal was prompt with the rent, intercourse between the two families was limited to formal greetings when
they happened to meet in the courtyard, which was of course
guarded by heavy iron bars on the street side. Héristal and
landlord shared a concierge, a brooding provincial, who after
years of living in Paris still refused to believe in it. And there
were never any complaints from the noble landlord, since
M. Héristal's celestial hobby was carried on at night and
silently. The passions of astronomy, however, are no less profound because they are not noisy.

The Héristal income was almost perfect of its kind for a
Frenchman. It derived from certain eastward-facing slopes near
Auxerre, on the Loire, on which the vines sucked the benevo-
lence from the early sun and avoided the poisons of the afternoon, and this, together with a fortunate soil and a cave of
perfect temperature, produced a white wine tasting like the
odor of spring wildflowers—a wine which, while it did not
travel well, had no need, for its devotees made pilgrimage to it.
This estate, while small, was perhaps the very best of a holding once very great. Furthermore, it was cultivated and nurtured by tenants expert to the point of magic, who moreover
paid their rent regularly and had, generation by generation.
M. Héristal's income was far from great, but it was constant
and it permitted him to live comfortably in the coach house of
Number One Avenue de Marigny; to attend carefully selected

plays, concerts, and ballet; to belong to a good social club and three learned societies; to purchase books as he needed them; and to peer as a respected amateur at the incredible heavens over the Eighth Arrondissement of Paris.

Indeed, if Pippin Héristal could have chosen the life he would most like to live, he would have spoken, with very few changes, for the life he was living in February of 19—. He was fifty-four, lean, handsome, and healthy in so far as he knew. By that I mean his health was so good that he was not aware he had it.

His wife, Marie, was a good wife and a good manager who knew her province and stayed in it. She was buxom and pleasant and under other circumstances might have taken her place at the bar of a very good small restaurant. Like most French-women of her class, she hated waste and heretics, considering the latter a waste of good heavenly material. She admired her husband without trying to understand him and had a degree of friendship with him which is not found in those marriages where passionate love sets torch to peace of mind. Her duty as she saw it was to keep a good, clean, economical house for her husband and her daughter, to do what she could about her liver, and to maintain the spiritual payments on her escrowed property in Heaven. These activities took up all her time. Her emotional overflow was absorbed by an occasional fight with the cook, Rose, and her steady warfare with wine-merchant and grocer, who were cheats and pigs, and, at certain times of the year, ancient camels. Madame's closest friend and perhaps only confidante was Sister Hyacinthe, of whom there will be more later.

M. Héristal was French of the French and yet French plus. For instance, he did not believe it was a sin not to speak French and an affectation for a Frenchman to learn other languages. He knew German, Italian, and English. He had a scholarly interest in progressive jazz, and he loved the cartoons in *Punch*. He admired the English for their intensity and their passion for roses, horses, and some kinds of conduct.

"An Englishman is a bomb," he would say, "but a bomb with a hidden fuse." He also observed, "Almost any generality

one makes about the English turns out at some time to be un-
true." And he would continue, "How different from the Americans they are!"

He knew and liked Cole Porter, Ludwig Bemelmans, and,
until a few years before, had known sixty per cent of the Harmonica Rascals. He had once shaken hands with Louis Arm-
strong and addressed him as Cher Maître Satchmo, to which
the master replied, "You frogs ape me."

The Héristal household was comfortable without being extrav-
agant, and carefully keyed to the family income, which was sufficient for the pleasant but frugal life which, as good French, Pippin
and Madame preferred to live. Monsieur's main extravagance
lay in the instruments of astronomy. His telescope of more than
amateur power was equipped with mounting of sufficient weight
and stability to overcome oscillation, and mechanism to com-
pensate for the earth's turning. Some of Pippin's celestial photographs have appeared in the magazine *Match,* and properly
so, for he is given credit for discovering the comet of 1951, designated the Elysée Comet. A Japanese amateur in California,
Walter Haschi, made a simultaneous report and shared credit
for the discovery. Haschi and Héristal still corresponded regularly and compared photographs and techniques.

Under ordinary circumstances Pippin read four daily papers
like any good and alert citizen. He was not political except in
so far as he distrusted all governments, particularly the one in
power, but this too might be said to be more French than individual.

The family Héristal was blessed with only one child—Clotilde,
twenty years old, intense, violent, pretty, and overweight. Her
background was interesting. At an early age she had revolted
against everything she could think of. At fourteen, Clotilde de-
termined to be a doctor of medicine; at fifteen she wrote a novel
entitled *Adieu Ma Vie,* which sold widely and was made into a
motion picture. As a result of her literacy and cinemagraphic
success she toured America and returned to France wearing
blue jeans, saddle oxfords, and a man's shirt, a style which instantly caught on with millions of gamines who for several
years were known as "Les Jeannes Bleues" and caused untold

pain to their parents. It was said that Les Jeannes Bleues were, if anything, sloppier and more frowzy than the Existentialists, while their stern-faced gyrations in le jitterbug caused many a French father to clench agonized fists over his head.

From the arts, Clotilde went directly into politics. At sixteen and a half she joined the Communists and held the all-time record of sixty-two hours of picketing the Citroën plant. It was during this association with the lower classes that Clotilde met Père Méchant, the little Pastor of the Pediment, who so impressed her that she seriously considered taking the veil in an order of nuns dedicated to silence, black bread, and pedicures for the poor. St. Hannah, patron saint of feet, founded the order.

On February 14, a celestial accident occurred which had a sharp effect on the Héristal household. A pre-equinoctial meteor shower put in an untimely and unpredicted appearance. Pippin worked frantically with the blazing heavens, exposing film after film, but even before he retired to his darkroom in the wine cellar off the stable he knew that his camera was not adequate to stop the fiery missiles in their flight. The developed film verified his fear. Cursing gently, he walked to a great optical supply house, conferred with the management, telephoned several learned friends. Then he strolled reluctantly back to Number One Avenue de Marigny, and so preoccupied was he that he did not notice the Gardes Républicains in shining cuirasses and red-plumed helmets, milling their horses around the gates of the Elysée Palace.

Madame was concluding an argument with Rose, the cook, as Pippin climbed the stairs. She emerged from the kitchen, victorious and a little red in the face, while the sullen muttering of the defeated Rose followed her down the hall.

In the salon she told her husband, "Closed the window over the cheese—a full kilogram of cheese suffocating all night with the window closed. And do you know what her excuse was? She was cold. For her own comfort the cheese must strangle. You can't trust servants anymore."

Monsieur said, "One finds oneself in a difficult situation."

"Difficult—of course it's difficult with the kind of trash who call themselves cooks—"

"Madame—the meteor shower continues. This is verified. I find I must procure a new camera."

The outgo of money was definitely in Madame's province. She remained silent, but Monsieur sensed danger in her narrowing eyes and in her hands, which rose slowly and saddled her hips.

He said uneasily, "It is a decision one must make. No one is to blame. One might say the order comes from Heaven itself."

Madame's voice was steel. "The cost of this—this camera, Monsieur?"

He named a price which shook her sturdy frame as though an internal explosion had occurred. But almost immediately she marshaled herself with iron discipline for the attack.

"Last month, M'sieur, it was a new—what do you call it? The expenditure for film is already ruinous. May I remind you, M'sieur, of the letter recently arrived from Auxerre, of the need for new cooperage, of the insistence that we stand half of the cost?"

"Madame," he cried, "I did not call down the meteor shower."

"Nor did I decay the casks at Auxerre."

"I have no choice, Madame."

She seemed to grow to a tower with castellations, and darkness hung about her like a personal thunderstorm.

"M'sieur is master of the house," she said. "If M'sieur wishes to allow the meteors to bring bankruptcy down on the heads of his family—who am I to complain? I must go to apologize to Rose. A kilo of strangulated cheese is a laughable nothing compared to the blobs of light on film. Can one eat meteors, M'sieur? Can one wear them to keep out the night damp? Can one make wine barrels of these precious meteors? M'sieur, I leave you to make your choice." And she moved on quiet, deadly feet out of the room.

Anger fought with panic in Pippin Héristal. Through the double glass doors he could see his telescope in its garment of waterproof silk. And anger won. He walked sternly down the stairs, crushed his hat on his head, took his stick from the rack and Clotilde's briefcase from the table. With furious dignity he crossed the courtyard and waited while the concierge opened the iron gate. In a moment of weakness he looked back and saw Madame watching him from the kitchen window and Rose scowling happily beside her.

"I am going to see Uncle Charlie," said Pippin Héristal, and he slammed the iron gate behind him.

Chalres Martel was proprietor of a small but prosperous art gallery and antique store in the Rue de Seine, a dark and pleasant place with pictures properly ill-lighted and provocative. He sold unsigned paintings which he would not guarantee as early Renoirs, and also bits of crystal, gilt, and chinoiserie which he could and did attest as coming from the great and ancient houses of France.

At the rear of the gallery a red velvet curtain concealed one of the most comfortable and discreet bachelor's quarters in all Paris. The chairs, softened by velvet cushions stuffed with down, were a joy to sit in. His bed, a triumph of Napoleonic work in gilded wood, had high curved head and foot like the prow and stern of a Viking dragon ship. During the day a cover and pillows made from softly faded altar cloths converted his sleeping arrangements into a charming nook, inviting and subtly sinful. Green-shaded lamps spread just enough light in the room to bring out beauties and to conceal defects. His cooking arrangements, a sink and a gas ring, were hidden behind a Chinese screen mellowed by the years to pearly black and melted butter. His bookcase was filled with leather and gold volumes, inviting to the eye without demanding that they be read.

Charles had always been a worldly man, gentle but inflexible, of impeccable carriage and dress. Now in his late sixties, he still adored ladies and his manner made ladies of all women until they insisted otherwise. Even now, when his impulse aimed more toward sleep than gallantry, he nevertheless kept his standard so high that selected young ladies felt a pleasant thrill on being invited past the red velvet curtain for an aperitif. And to the best of Charles's ability, they were not disappointed. A little door opened on an alleyway behind the shop—a small thing, but one to give his companions confidence.

When the custodian of an ancient name and a bat-ridden château required a relaxing day at Auteuil or a new lining for a fur-collared topcoat, where was there a better place to take the crystal chandelier from the ballroom or the inlaid piquet table once the property of a king's mistress than to the gallery of Uncle Charlie? And a chosen group of customers understood that, if pressed, Charles Martel could come up with a rarity. Willie Chitling, the movie producer, built the entire bar in his ranch house at Palm Springs with the furniture, paneling, and thirteenth-century altar from the chapel of the Château Vieilleculotte. Charles also made reasonable loans. He was said to hold the personal IOUs of nine out of the Twelve Peers of France.

Charles Martel was the uncle and friend of Pippin Arnulf Héristal. He went out of his field of art and bric-a-brac to trace the Bix Beiderbecke records for Pippin's almost perfect collection. Also he was his nephew's adviser in matters spiritual and temporal.

When M. Héristal stormed into the gallery in the Rue de Seine, Charles noted that he had come in a taxi. The mission was therefore serious.

Charles gestured his nephew past the velvet curtain and quickly concluded the sale of a Louis Quinze make up box to an elderly lady tourist for whom it had no practical value. He closed the negotiation not by lowering the price but by suddenly raising it, which convinced the lady that she should buy it at once or she wouldn't get it at all. Charles bowed her out of the gallery, shut the front door, and hung a battered card which read "Closed for Renovation." Then he himself went past the velvet curtain and greeted his pacing nephew.

"You are troubled, my child," he said. "Sit down, sit down. Let me give you a drop of cognac for your nerves."

"I am in a fury," Pippin said, but he did sit down and he did accept the cognac.

"It is Marie?" said Uncle Charlie. "Or perhaps Clotilde?"

"It is Marie."

"It is about money?"

"It is about money," said Pippin.

"How much?"

"I did not come to borrow."

"You come, then, to complain?"

"Exactly, to complain."

"A good idea. It removes pressures. You will return to your home in a more agreeable humor, in a word a better husband. Do you wish to be specific in your complaint?"

Pippin said, "An unpredicted meteor shower has blundered into earth's atmosphere. My camera is not adequate to—well, I need a new camera."

"Expensive, and Marie does not find it necessary?"

"You understand the situation very well. She wears her hurt look, that damnable injured expression. She is planning revenge."

"You have bought the camera?"

"Not yet."

"But you have decided."

"Understand, my uncle, it is unusual to find showers of meteors at this season. Who knows what is going on up there? Do not forget that it was I who first reported the Elysée Comet. I was commended by the Academy. It is whispered that in the not too distant future I may be elected."

"Congratulations, my child. What an honor! While I myself do not view the heavens with passion, I support passion, whatever its source. Begin your complaint, my dear nephew. Now— I am Marie and you are you. Shall we start with the undeniable fact that your income springs from your property, rather than from *dot*?"

"Exactly."

"This land has belonged to your family since the dawn of history."

"Since the Salic Franks invaded from the east."

"In very truth your vineyard hills are the remains of a kingdom."

"An empire."

"You stem from a family so ancient, so noble, that you do not condescend to remind the upstart nobility of your origin by use of titles clearly yours."

"You put it very well, Uncle Charlie. And all I want is a new camera."

"There," said Charles. "You feel better now?"

"I really do."

"Let me lend you the money for the camera, my child. You can pay it back little by little. Marie does not shy at little things—it is large expenditures which frighten and confuse her."

"I did not come to borrow."

"You have not asked. I have offered. You will purchase the camera. You will inform Marie that you have decided not to buy it. Does Marie know one camera from another?"

"Of course not. But will I not have surrendered my position in the house?"

"Quite the contrary, my child. You will have put her in a position of guilt. She will urge you to buy many little things. Thus you will repay the loan."

"I wonder you have never married."

"I prefer to see other people happy. Now—for what amount shall I make the check?"

When M. Héristal had slammed the iron gate and stormed to the taxi rank on Avenue Gabriel, Madame, for all her cold and deadly triumph, was shaken and uncertain—and at such times it was her habit to visit her old friend Sister Hyacinthe in her convent not far from the Porte de Vincennes—a large, low, orderly building within sight of the Bois. Madame changed her dress, took purse and black shopping bag, and took the métro.

Sister Hyacinthe had been her childhood friend and moreover they had gone to school together. Suzanne Lescault was a pretty child, with a thin, true singing voice and a natural ability as a dancer so that she dominated the pageants and little plays of the school. Inevitably Suzanne rose from wood sprite to fairy queen to Pierrette, and later, for three successive years, she acted *Joan the Maid* to the complete satisfaction of its authoress, the Sister Superior. And Marie, who could neither sing nor dance, far from being jealous, adored her gifted friend and felt that she somehow participated in her triumphs.

In the normal course of events Suzanne would have married and retired her talents and her blossoming figure. However, a distant manipulation of the Crédit Lyonnais and the subsequent suicide of her father, an officer in that organization, left Suzanne with a sickly mother, a dwarflike schoolboy brother in a black smock, and the necessity for making her way in the world. Only then did the often heard comment that she should be on the stage make some sense to Suzanne and more to her mother.

The Comédie Française had no immediate openings but took her name, and while she waited Suzanne was employed by the Folies Bergère, where her voice, her grace, and her high and perfect bosom were instantly appreciated and utilized. Her mother's professional illness, and her brother's interminable education, followed by his death by misadventure with a motorcycle, made it economically unsound for Suzanne to jeopardize a permanent and well-paid position for the uncertainty of higher art.

For many years she graced the stage of the Folies, not only in the line of lovely undressed girls, but also with speaking, singing, and dancing parts. After twenty years of complicated and complaining illness, her mother died without a single symptom. By this time Suzanne had become not only a performer but ballet mistress.

She was very tired. Her bosom had remained high; her arches had fallen. She had lived a life of comparative virtue, as do most Frenchwomen. Indeed it is a matter of disillusion to young male Americans otherwise informed, to discover that the French are a moral people—judged, that is, by American country-club standards.

Suzanne wanted to rest her feet. She left a world about which she knew perhaps too much and after a proper novitiate took the veil as Sister Hyacinthe in an order of contemplation which demanded a great deal of sitting down.

As a nun Sister Hyacinthe radiated such peace and piety that she became an ornament to her order, while her knowledge and background made her both tolerant and helpful to younger sisters with troubles.

During all the years of both her lives she had maintained contact with her old school friend Marie. Even between visits they kept up a detailed and dull correspondence, exchanging complaints and recipes. Marie still adored her talented and now saintly friend. It was perfectly natural that she called upon her in the matter of the camera.

In the tidy and comfortable little visiting room of the convent near Vincennes, Marie said, "I am at my wit's end. In most things M'sieur is as considerate as one could wish, but where his ill-named stars are concerned he pours out money like water."

Sister Hyacinthe smiled at her. "Why don't you beat him?" she asked pleasantly.

"Pardon? Oh! I see you make a jollity. I assure you it is a serious matter. The cooperage at Auxerre—"

"Is there food on the table, Marie? Is the rent paid? Have they cut off the electricity?"

"It is a matter of principle and of precedent," said Marie a little stiffly.

"My dear friend," said the nun, "did you come to me for advice or to complain?"

"Why, for advice of course. I never complain."

"Of course not," said Sister Hyacinthe, and she continued softly, "I have known many people to ask for advice but very few who wanted it and none who followed it. However, I will advise you."

"Please do," said Marie distantly.

"In my profession, Marie, I have had contacts with many men. I think I am in a position to make some generalities about them. First, they are like children, sometimes spoiled children."

"Now there I agree with you."

"The ones who really truly grow up, Marie, are no good because men are either children or old—there is nothing in between. But in their childlike unreason and irresponsibility there is sometimes greatness. Please understand that I know most women are more intelligent, but women grow up, women face realities—and women are very rarely great. One of the few regrets I have in my present profession is the lack of male non-sense. It at least makes for contrast," said Sister Hyacinthe.

"He discovered a comet," said Marie. "The Academy commended him. But this new camera business—that goes too far."

"Again I ask—do you want my advice?"

"Of course."

"Then advise him to buy the camera—insist on it."

"But I have already taken my stand. I would lose his respect."

"On the contrary," said Sister Hyacinthe, "if you should advise the expenditure, even suggest a greater one, you might find a reluctance on his part to spend the money. He might then have to inspect realities instead of simply opposing you. They are very curious creatures, men."

"I've brought you some handkerchiefs," said Marie.

"Oh, how beautiful! Marie, there is genius in your fingers. How do your eyes permit this tiny embroidery?"

"My eyes have always been good," said Marie.

When Madame returned to Number One Avenue de Marigny she found the double doors of the salon open and her husband busy with small shining tools at his telescope.

"I have been thinking," she said. "It occurs to me that you should buy the camera."

"Eh?" he said.

"Why, it might mean your election to the Academy."

"You are kind," said her husband. "But I too have been thinking. First things must come first. No, I will get along with what I have."

"I implore you."

"No," he said.

"I command it."

"My dear, let us not be confused about who is the head of this house. Do not let us, like the Americans, hear the hens crowing."

"Forgive me," said Marie.

"It is nothing, Madame. And now I must prepare for the

night. The meteor shower continues, my dear. The stars have no interest in our problems."

From the floor above came a metallic crash. M. Héristal looked up apprehensively. "I didn't know Clotilde was in."

"The copper table in the hallway," said Madame. "It leaps out at her. I must put it somewhere else."

"Please don't allow her on the terrace, Marie," he said. "My telescope might leap at her."

Clotilde sauntered down the stairs, her dress a little tight over her growing inches. A sullen-looking little fur, savagely biting its own tail, hung limply from her shoulders.

"You are going out, my dear?" Madame asked.

"Oh, yes, Maman. I am having a screen test."

"Not another one!"

"One does as one's director suggests," said Clotilde.

M'sieur moved protectively in front of his telescope as his daughter glided through the double doors and tripped slightly on the doorstep.

"You have then a director?" he asked.

"They are casting for the novel *The Ragamuffin Princess.* You see, there's an orphaned girl and—"

"And she finds out she is a princess. It is an American novel."

"You have read it?"

"No, my dear, but I know it."

"How do you know it is American?"

"For one thing because the Americans have perhaps an exaggerated interest in princesses, and for another thing they have a strong feeling for the Cinderella story."

"Cinderella?"

"You should read it, my dear," he said.

"Gregory Peck is going to play the prince."

"Of course he is," said M'sieur. "Now if it were a French novel the princess would find out that— Careful, my dear— please don't come near the telescope. It is arranged for tonight's show."

When their daughter had oozed away down the stairs and

the gate to the courtyard had clanged behind her, Madame said, "I liked it almost better when she was writing novels. She was at home more often. In a way I will be glad when she finds a nice boy of a good family."

"She must be a princess first," said her husband. "Everyone must."

"You should not make fun of her."

"Perhaps I was not. I can remember such dreams. They were very real."

"You are amiable, M'sieur."

"I am curiously excited and content, Marie. For a whole week I shall be entertained"—he raised his fingers lightly—"by my friends up there."

"And you will be up all night and sleep all day."

"Of a certainty," said M. Héristal.

The events of 19— in France should be studied not for their uniqueness but rather for their inevitability. The study of history, while it does not endow with prophecy, may indicate lines of probability.

It was and is no new thing for a French government to fall for lack of a vote of confidence. What has been called in other countries "instability" is in France a kind of stability. Lord Cotten has said that "In France anarchy has been refined to the point of reaction," and later, "Stability to a Frenchman is intolerable tyranny." Alas, too few are emotionally capable of understanding Lord Cotten.

Many millions of words partisan and passionate have been written about the recent French crisis and re-crisis. It remains to trace the process with the cool and appraising eye of the historian.

On February 12, 19—, when M. Rumorgue was finally placed in the position of asking for a vote on the issue of Monaco, it is conceded that he knew the result in advance. Indeed, there were many around him who felt he welcomed the termination of his premiership. M. Rumorgue, in addition to his titular

leadership of the Proto-Communist party, which is traditionally two degrees right of center, is an authority in psycho-
botany. To accept the premiership at all, he had reluctantly
abandoned for the time being the experiments concerning pain
in plants which he had been carrying on for many years at his
nursery at Juan les Pins. Few people outside this field are even
aware of Professor Rumorgue's Separate entitled *Tendencies
and Symptoms of Hysteria in Red Clover,* reprinted from his
address to the Academy of Horticulture. His academic triumph
over his critics, some of whom went to the extreme of denouncing him as being crazier than his clover, must have made
him doubly reluctant to assume not only the leadership of his
party but also the premiership of France. The newspaper *Peace
Thru War,* although in opposition to the Proto-Communists,
very likely quoted M. Rumorgue correctly in remarking that
white clover with all its faults was easier to deal with emotionally than the elected representatives of the people of France.

The question on which M. Rumorgue's government failed,
while interesting, was not nationally important. It is widely be-
lieved that if the Monaco question had not arisen, some other
difficulty would have taken its place. M. Rumorgue himself
emerged with honor and was able to work quietly on his forthcoming book on "Inherited Schizophrenia in Legumes"—a
group of Mendelian by-laws.

At any rate, France found herself without a government. It
will be remembered that when President Sonnet called on the
Christian Atheists to form a government they could not agree
even within their own ranks. Likewise the Socialists failed to
draw support. The Christian Communists, with the support of
the Non-Tax-Payers' League, failed to qualify. Only then did
M. Sonnet call the historic conference of leaders of all parties at
the Elysée Palace.

The parties involved at this time should be listed, since some
of them have since disappeared and been replaced by others.
Those groups attending the president's call are here listed, not
by their power but simply geographically in relation to the center. Gathered in the Elysée Palace were:

The Conservative Radicals
The Radical Conservatives
The Royalists
The Right Centrists
The Left Centrists
The Christian Atheists
The Christian Christians
The Christian Communists
The Proto-Communists
The Neo-Communists
The Socialists
    and
The Communists

The Communists were broken up into:

Stalinists
Trotskyists
Khrushchevniks
Bulganinians

For three days the struggle raged. The leaders slept on the brocade couches of the Grand Ballroom and subsisted on the bread and cheese and Algerian wine furnished by M. le Président. It was a scene of activity and turmoil. The Elysée Ballroom is not only wainscoted with mirrors but also has mirrors on its ceiling, which created the impression that instead of forty-two party chiefs there were literally thousands. Every raised fist became fifty fists, while the echo from the hard mirror surfaces threw back the sounds of a multitude.

M. Rumorgue, the fallen minister and leader of the Proto-Communists, left the meeting and went back to Juan les Pins on receipt of a telegram from Madame Rumorgue saying that the Poland China sow, named Anxious, had farrowed.

At the end of seven days the conference had accomplished nothing. President Sonnet put the Elysée bathroom at the disposal of the delegates, at the same time refusing to be responsible for their linen.

The seriousness of the impasse at last began to be reflected in the Paris press. The humorous periodical *Alligator* suggested that the situation should be made permanent, since no national crisis had arisen since the party leaders were taken out of circulation.

Great historic decisions often result from small and even flippant causes. Well into the second week, the leaders of the larger political parties found that their voices, which had gone from loud to harsh to hoarse, were finally disappearing completely.

It was at this time that the compact group of the leaders of the Royalist party took the floor. Having had no hope of being included in any new government, they had abstained from making speeches, and thus had kept their voices. After the confusion of eight days of meetings, the calm of the Royalists was by contrast explosive.

The Comte de Terrefranque advanced to the rostrum and took the floor in spite of an impassioned but whispered address by M. Triflet, the Radical Conservative.

M. le Comte in a clear, loud voice announced that the Royalist group had joined forces. He himself, he said, in spite of his basic and unchanging loyalty to the Merovingian line, from which his title derived, had agreed to join the Bourbons, not from lack of respect and love for his own great tradition, but simply because the Merovingians were not able to produce a prince of clear and direct descent. He therefore introduced the Duc des Troisfronts, whose proposal would have the backing not only of the other Royalist parties but also of the noble and intelligent people of France.

The Duc des Troisfronts, who under ordinary circumstances was shielded from public appearances, because of the split palate which has been his family's chief characteristic for many generations, now took the stand and was able to make himself not only heard but even understood.

France, he said, stood at the crossroads. Under the tattered flag of the unwashed, the greedy, and the inept, France had seen herself reduced from the glorious leadership of the world to a bitter, bickering, third-rate power, a craven province trying unsuccessfully to lick the boots of England and the United States on the one hand—or rather foot—and of the Commissars on the other.

M. le Duc was so surprised that he had been able to say all of this that he sat down and had to be reminded that he had not arrived at the point. Once reminded, however, he graciously arose again. He suggested, even commanded, that the monarchy be restored so that France might rise again like the phoenix out of the ashes of the Republic to cast her light over the world. He ended his address in tears and immediately left the room, crying to the Gardes Républicains at the gates of the palace, "I have failed! I have failed!" But, indeed, as everyone knows, he had not failed.

The announcement by the Duc des Troisfronts had the effect of shocking the party leaders to silence. Every man seemed frozen within himself. Only very gradually did a series of whispered conferences begin. Party leaders collected in knots and spoke together in low tones, glancing occasionally over their shoulders.

M. Deuxcloches, actual leader of the Communist bloc, although he himself holds only the humble party position of Cultural Custodian, seems to have been the first to realize the implications of the proposal of des Troisfronts.

At M. Deuxcloches' behest, the Communist group left the ballroom and reassembled in the president's bathroom. But here a protocolic impasse arose. Two officials were involved, and two seats. M. Douxpied was indeed party Secretary, but Cultural Custodian Deuxcloches was conceded to hold the actual power. This being so, the question arose as to which took precedence, toilet or bidet? Such a consideration might have engaged the meeting indefinitely had not M. Gustave Harmonie flung himself passionately into the breach. It was true, he argued, that the Communist party was the Communist party, but, he continued—France was France.

M. Deuxcloches stroked his chin nervously and made his historic choice by taking his position on the bidet. However, in view of possible review, he held that the apparent deviation was only local. The German party, he maintained, might feel called upon to take an opposite course. The burst of applause at his decision gave him courage to go on.

M. Deuxcloches argued as follows. The Communist party's natural function was revolution, he said. Any change which made revolution more feasible was undeniably to the party's advantage. French politics were in a state of anarchy. It is very difficult to revolt against anarchy, since in the popular mind, undialectically informed, revolution *is* anarchy. There is no point, to the uninstructed, in substituting anarchy for anarchy. On the other hand, he continued, monarchy is the natural magnet for revolution, as can be historically verified. Therefore, it would be to the Communists' advantage if the French monarchy were restored. That would be a position to kick off from and, indeed, would speed up the revolution.

M. Douxpied broke in at this juncture to point out that world opinion might be startled to find the French Communist party advocating the return of a king.

M. Deuxcloches assured the party Secretary that no such report would go out. The French party would not vote at all. Once the king was crowned, it would be time to announce that France had been misled by unkept promises and imperialist pressures. Meanwhile, definite work toward the revolution could proceed.

After a few moments of thought, M. Douxpied arose and warmly clasped the hand of M. Deuxcloches, a simple and symbolic gesture of agreement. The other members instantly followed suit. However, one delegate did suggest that perhaps, with the Communists abstaining, the Socialists might join the Christian Atheists and the Proto-Communists to defeat the measure.

"Then we must make sure they do not," M. Deuxcloches replied. "If the Socialists do not think of it themselves it might be suggested to them that a king would keep the Communists in check."

His statement drew applause and the meeting adjourned back to the Ballroom.

Meanwhile, there had been other conferences among other partisans. The Socialists, for example, did not need any suggestion. It was obvious to them that a king would indeed keep the

Communists in check. With that stumbling block out of the way, the Socialists could look forward to the gradual change which was their advocation.

The Christian Atheists agreed together that under the present scattering of parties, with resulting confusion, the unconfused Church was making inroads. Monarchy, on the other hand, was the natural enemy of the Church Militant; England was the perfect example of popular monarchy's successful stand against inroads of Rome.

The Christian Christians took the position that the royal family had always been unequivocally Catholic, while the aristocracy, particularly those members stemming from the Ancien Régime, if they had not deviated in adversity would not be likely to do so once their dream had come true.

The Left Centrists are a powerful force, particularly when they are able to find a common ground with the Right Centrists. Together these parties represent what have been called the Hundred Families, although since the Second World War and American economic aid, they might be better designated as the Two Hundred Families. These two parties represent not only mining and manufacturing, but also banking and insurance and real estate, the only difference between them being that the Left Centrists favor retirement and medical provisions common to American corporations, while the Right Centrists do not. These two parties were able to agree almost immediately on restoration of the monarchy, because a king would undoubtedly curb both Socialists and Communists and in so doing would put an end to demands for pay increases and shorter hours.

The Non-Tax-Payers' League concluded that a Royalist regime would collect taxes from Right and Left Centrists, and this was their main reason for being. They were quite aware that the projected monarchy would not collect taxes from the aristocracy, but they argued that this was a very small group and moreover bankrupt so that it was not important if Royalists were exempt.

There grew up a unanimity of direction among the political parties unique in recent history. Each group favored the restora-

tion of the monarchy for different reasons and for reasons bene-
ficial to itself. The Communists, true to their position, maintained
a sullen silence.

The debate caught fire in the French press, which found, in
increased circulation, its own reasons for keeping the matter in
the public eye. *Le Figaro,* in a front-page editorial, argued that
French dignity and integrity would be better served if its symbol were a king rather than a dressmaker. The Parisians in general favored a proposal which promised variety, while the
Association of Restaurateurs, the Couture, and the Hotel Association felt that, since Americans loved royalty, the increase
in tourism and spending alone would justify the change. As for
the farmers, provincial and peasant, they are traditionally op-
posed to any government in power and so are automatically in
favor of change, good or bad. In the National Assembly the en-
thusiasts demanded an immediate vote.

The Royalists of France, or for that matter of any country
where royalty has been eliminated as a governing principle,
have never given up. Indeed, it is a part of the nature, even of
the triumphant gallantry of an aristocracy, that it does not, it
cannot, abandon the certainty of its return, bringing with it the
golden days, the prosperous and courteous days. Then again
will come honor and truthfulness, devotion to duty and rever-
ence for the king; then will servants and peasants be protected
and sheltered, not turned out into a rapacious world; then will
a man be properly known for his illustrious past rather than for
his aggressive and greedy present; then will Gracious Majesty
preside like a benevolent umpire over the refined and well-
born. The king will tenderly direct and correct proper families
and sternly reproach and punish any who attempt to force
themselves in or to change the rules. Then will gentlemen be
gallant to ladies and ladies lovely and gracious to gentlemen.
Anyone who does not hold these things to be true has no place
in the ranks of the noblesse.

The Royalists were a clot in the bloodstream of the Republic. The Royalist party, while not numerous, rich, nor vocal, was
close-knit and passionately devoted. Any difficulties among its

members were social or had to do with ancient prestige and the maintenance of a permanently fragile honor.

While the National Assembly debated the return of the monarchy with increasing fervor and approval, the Royalists met in a hall which had once housed the Czech Social Gymnastic and Oratory Club and had been abandoned after the *Anschluss* with the Soviet Union.

No one could have foreseen any difficulty. The Bourbon Pretender was available, legitimate, and trained for his position. Fortunately, he had not been asked to the meeting. There were present:

> Vercingetorians
> Merovingians
> Carolingians
> Capetians
> Burgundians
> Orleanists
> Bourbons
> Bonapartists

And two very small groups—

Angevins, who were rumored to have British support, and
Caesarians, who claimed their descent from Julius and
    bore the bend sinister proudly.

The Bourbons walked like emperors and smiled little Bourbon smiles when the king's health was drunk. But when they named their Pretender, the Comte de Paris—all hell broke loose.

Bonapartists leaped up, their eyes wild. Comte de Jour, whose great-grandfather had carried his marshal's baton in his knapsack, cried "Bourbon! Why Bourbon? Has the sacred blood of Napoleon run out? And aligned with Orleans? Gentlemen, are we to live under the shadow of Bourbon and Orleans, the two lines which contributed most to the fall of the French monarchy? Are we—?"

"No," screamed the Angevins, with what some thought was an English accent.

"Better the Merovingians, better the Rois Fainéants," shrieked the Capetians.

For a day and a night the battle raged while noble voices grew hoarse and noble hearts pounded. Of all the aristocratic partisans, only the Merovingians sat back, quiet, listless, content, and faint.

It was mid-morning of the second day when exhaustion proclaimed to all the undeniable fact that the Royalists could no more settle on a king than the Republicans could form a government. In the night they had sent for a sheaf of swords and altered the Code by acclamation. Hardly a gentleman there was who did not wear scratches and cuts which proclaimed that his honor was intact. Only the lazy Merovingians were unruffled and unscarred.

At 10:37 A.M., February 21, 19—, the elderly Childéric de Saône stood gradually up and spoke softly in his dusty Merovingian voice, which nevertheless was one of the few voices left.

"My noble friends," he began, "as you know, I adhere to a dynasty which does not admit that you exist."

A Bourbon lunged tiredly toward the umbrella stand of swords, but Childéric stopped him with an upraised hand.

"Desist, dear Marquis," he said. "My kings, it is recorded, disappeared through lassitude. We Merovingians do not want the crown. Consequently, perhaps we are in a position to arbitrate—to advise." He smiled wanly. "It appears to us that the Republican years have left their mark on this gathering. You, sirs, have conducted yourselves with all the foolishness of the elected representatives of an even less endowed populace but without their endurance. I am glad that this has been a closed meeting so that no one could see us."

A guilty silence fell on the gathering. The nobles hung their heads in shame while Childéric continued.

"In the days of my ancestors," he said, "these matters of succession were handled in a nobler manner—with poison, poniard, or the quick and merciful hands of the strangler. Now we have surrendered to the ballot. Very well, let us use it like noblemen. Let him who can vote most often, win."

Childéric paused, unscrewed the handle of his walking stick, and took a sip of the cognac which replaced the blade the stick had once concealed.

"Is anyone ready to interrupt me now?" he asked courteously. "Very well, I will continue. It seems apparent that Bourbon, Orleans, Burgundy, even cadet Capet, can only reign by the old method of decimation. I suggest, therefore, that we go further back. As for Anjou—" He spread his first and second fingers in the Churchill victory sign but pointed them forward, which alters the meaning of the gesture.

Burgundy leaped up, intending to shout, "Who? You?" but the bleat his tortured throat emitted sounded more like, "Whee? Yee?"

"No," said Childéric, "I am content to live as my latter kings lived and to solve the problem as they did. I suggest for the throne of France the holy blood of Charlemagne."

Bourbon exploded in a thunderous whisper. "Are you insane? The line has disappeared."

"Not so," said Childéric quietly. "You will recall, noble sirs, although at the time your ancestors were herding sheep, that Pippin II of Héristal, ignoring the Salic custom of partition, gave all his realm to his son Charles—later called the Hammer."

"What of it?" Bourbon demanded. "There is no issue now."

"Not from Charles Martel, no. But I ask you also to remember that Charles was illegitimate. Perhaps this has blinded you to the fact that Pippin II had two legitimate sons and these he passed over *de jeure*, but could he, did he have the power *in esse* or *de facto*?

"In Paris today lives Pippin Arnulf Héristal, a pleasant man, an amateur astronomer, while his Uncle Charles Martel is proprietor of a small gallery in the Rue de Seine. Being descended from the legitimate branch, perhaps he uses the name Martel improperly."

"But can they prove it?"

"They can prove it," Childéric assured the nobles pleasantly. "Pippin is an old friend of mine. He is clever. He balances my checkbook. I call him the Mayor of the Palace—a poor joke, but we laugh. Pippin lives on the proceeds of two vineyards, the last remnant of the monster estates of Héristal and Arnulf. Noble sirs, I have the honor to propose that we unite under His Gracious Majesty Pippin of Héristal and Arnulf, of the line of Charlemagne."

The die was cast, although the whispering went on until weary evening proved that no other agreement was possible.

Finally the nobility concurred. They even tried to cheer—to cheer the king. They succeeded in drinking his health and they carried the name and origin of Pippin to the floor of the National Assembly, where it was received with relieved enthusiasm, for it had already occurred to the more astute representatives of the French people that 1789 was not so long ago. But who could hate Héristal—or Charlemagne?

Under ordinary circumstances M. Héristal kept himself informed of the activities and processes of government. However, the double excitement of the meteor shower and the triumphant intricacy of the new camera kept him on the roof terrace at night and in the wine-cellar darkroom in the morning, wherefrom he retired, exhausted but happy, to recuperate for the next evening.

M. Héristal was one of the very few in France, perhaps in the world, who were not aware that the Republic had been voted out of existence and the French monarchy proclaimed. It follows that he was also ignorant that he himself had been elected by acclamation King of France with the name Pippin IV. Pippin the Short, son of Charles Martel, who died in 768 A.D., was considered to have been Pippin III.

When the triumphant committee bore the official will of the people of France to the house at Number One Avenue de Marigny at nine o'clock in the morning, M. Héristal, in wine-colored dressing gown, was sitting in his study, drinking a cup of hot Sanka imported from America and preparing to go to bed.

He listened courteously, removing his pince-nez and rubbing his reddened eyes. At first he was wearily amused. But when he realized that the suggestion was serious he was deeply shocked. He placed his pince-nez astraddle his right forefinger, where it rode like a saddle.

"Gentlemen," he said, "you are making a joke, and, if you will excuse my observation, a joke not in good taste."

His unbelief increased the vehemence of the committee. They shouted with renewed voices. They demanded his instant acceptance of the throne for the safety and the future of France.

In the midst of the tumult, Pippin leaned back in his chair and put his blue-veined hand to his forehead as though to shut the unreal scene away.

"Sometimes," he said, "a man imagines things, particularly when he is fatigued. I do hope, gentlemen, that when I open my eyes you will not be here. I will then take something for my liver."

"But Your Majesty—"

Pippin's eyes popped open. "Oh, well," he said. "There was just a chance. That term 'Your Majesty' makes me uneasy. I must believe, I suppose, that you gentlemen are not playing some complicated practical joke—no, you do not appear to be joking types—but if you are not insane, what is your authority for this ridiculous proposal?"

M. Flosse of the Right Centrists put an oratorical edge to his voice. "France has found it impossible to form a government, Sire. For a number of years governments have fallen as soon as they have agreed on a policy."

"I know," said Pippin. "Perhaps policy is what we are afraid of."

M. Flosse went on. "France needs a continuity to ride secure above party and above faction. Look at England! Parties may change in England but there is a direction inherent in the monarchy. This France once had. This France has lost. We believe, Your Majesty, that it can be restored."

Pippin said softly, "England's monarchs lay cornerstones and take unequivocal positions on the kind of hat to wear to a racetrack. But have you thought, my friends, that Englishmen love their government and spend most of their time celebrating it, while Frenchmen on the contrary automatically detest any gov-

ernment in power? I am of the same persuasion. It is the French
way of regarding government. Until I am better informed, I
would like to go to sleep. But have you thought of the difficulties involved in your—plan? France has been a republic for
some time now. Her institutions are republican, her thinking is
republican. I think I had better go to bed. You still haven't told
me who sent this deputation."

M. Flosse cried, "The Senate and the Assembly of France
only await Your Majesty's gracious acceptance. We are sent by
the representatives of the people of France."

"Will the Communists vote for the monarchy?" Héristal
asked gently.

"They will not oppose, Sire. They guarantee that."

"And how about the people of France? I seem to remember
that they swarmed into Paris with pitchforks and that some
royalty—fortunately no relatives of mine—did not survive."

Senator Veauvache, the Socialist, rose to his feet. This is the
same Veauvache who aroused national attention in 1948 by refusing a bribe. At that time he was given the honorary title
Honnête Jean, which he has carried with humility to this day.
M. Veauvache said solemnly, "A sampling of opinion indicates
that the French people will unite behind you as one man."

"Whom did you sample?" Pippin asked.

"That is beside the point," Honnête Jean said. "In America,
the home of the opinion poll, does anyone ask that insulting
question?"

"I'm sorry," Pippin apologized. "I guess it is because I am
sleepy and confused and tired. I am not as young as I was—"

"Poof!" said M. Flosse flatteringly.

"And, too, I have been busy with—" He gestured upward.
"Madame doesn't bother me with news when I am preoccupied. You see, gentlemen, I am taken off guard."

"You must be crowned at Reims," cried M. Flosse, and his
eyes brimmed with emotion. "We must follow the old customs.
France needs you, Sire. Will you deny your country the security
of your great bloodline?"

"My bloodline?"

"Are you not directly descended from Pippin the Second?"

"Oh! Is that what it's all about? But there have been so many other royal houses since—"

"But you do not deny your descent?"

"How could I? I believe it is a matter of record."

"Do you forbid us, Sire?"

"That's silly," said Pippin. "How can I forbid anything a republic might take it into its head to do, even destroy itself? I am the broken tip of a long dog's long tail. Can I wag that dog?"

"France needs—"

"And I need sleep, gentlemen. Please leave me now and I will awaken some hours hence, hoping that you have been a dream."

And while he slept what has been called in the press the "Historic Nap," students from the Sorbonne marched up the Champs Elysées, shouting "Vive le roi!" and "Saint Denis pour la France." Four of them climbed the girders of the Eiffel Tower and raised an antique royal standard on the very top, where it fluttered triumphantly among the wind gauges.

The citizens boiled into the streets, dancing and singing with excitement.

Barrels of wine from the cooperative warehouses up-Seine were rolled through the streets and broached on the street corners.

The Lords of the Couture rushed to their drawing boards.

Schiaparelli, within the house, announced a new perfume called "Rêve Royale."

Special editions of *L'Espèce, Cormoran, Paris Minuit, L'Era,* and *Monde Dieu* rolled from the presses and were snatched up.

The royal standard of Charlemagne appeared like magic in shop windows.

The American Ambassador, with instructions from his government, sought in vain for someone to congratulate.

The wave overflowed Paris, and concentric circles spread into the provinces, lighting bonfires and raising flags.

And through it all, the king slept. But Madame made hourly visits to the kiosk for the new editions and piled them neatly on his desk for his perusal.

Pippin might well have slept through the night and into the

next day had not the anti-aircraft batteries disposed about
Paris fired a royal salute at two-thirty in the morning. Five citizens were killed and thirty-two were wounded by the fallback.
The thirty-two wounded made loyal and enthusiastic state-
ments from their hospital beds.

The firing of the anti-aircraft guns awakened Pippin. His first
thought was, It must be Clotilde coming in. What has she
stumbled over now?

A second salvo of anti-aircraft guns brought him up on his
elbow, his left hand thrashing about, seeking the bed reading
light. "Marie!" he called. "Marie! What is that?"

Madame opened the door. Her arms were loaded with newspapers. "It is the Royal Salute," she said. "*L'Espèce* says there
will be one hundred and one guns."

"My God!" said Pippin. "I thought it was Clotilde." He
looked at his watch, then raised his voice to be heard over the
guns. "It is three, less fifteen minutes. Where is Clotilde?"

Madame said coldly, "La Princesse, on a motor scooter, is
leading her loyal subjects to Versailles. She is going to start the
fountains."

Pippin said, "Then it was no dream! When the Minister of
Public Works hears of this, I smell the guillotine. Marie, these
people seem to mean this nonsense. I want to talk to Uncle
Charlie."

In the early dawn the king and his uncle faced each other in the
rear of the gallery in the Rue de Seine.

Pippin had battered on the shutters of Charles Martel's establishment until that gentleman, clad in a long nightgown and
a tarboosh, ill-tempered with sleep, peered out at him. After a
time of grumbling, of making his morning chocolate, and of
pulling on his trousers, Uncle Charlie settled back on his dusty
Morocco armchair, adjusted the green-shaded reading light,
polished his glasses, and prepared for business.

"You must study calmness, Pippin," he said. "For years I
have recommended calmness. When you burst in here with

your ——— comet, I suggested that the stars would wait on a cup of chocolate. When Clotilde had her small difficulty with the gendarmes about the improper use of firearms at the shooting gallery, did I not recommend calm? And it came out all right, you remember. You paid for a few light globes she shot from a carousel, and Clotilde sold her life story to an American magazine. Calm! Pippin. Calm! I recommend calm."

"But they have gone insane, Uncle Charlie."

"No, my boy, abandon that theory. The French do not go insane unless there is some advantage in it. Now you say that the delegation was composed of all parties, and you further say that they mentioned the future well-being of France."

"They say France must have a stable government."

"Hmmm," said Uncle Charlie. "It has always seemed to me that this is the last thing they want. It is possible, Pippin, that the parties have chosen a direction, but for different reasons. Yes, that must be it, and you, my poor boy, have been chosen for the role of what the Americans call a 'patsy.'"

"What can I do, Uncle Charlie? How can I avoid this—this patsy?"

Uncle Charlie tapped his glasses on his knee, sneezed, poured himself a fresh cup of chocolate from the saucepan on the gas ring at his elbow, and slowly shook his head.

"With time and calm," he said, "I could possibly work out the political background. But right at the moment I cannot see any escape for you unless you wish to retire with dignity to a warm bath and cut your wrists."

"I don't want to be king!"

"If suicide does not appeal to you, dear boy, you may relax in the certainty that in the near future there will be attempts at assassination and, who knows, one of them may succeed."

"Can't I say no, Uncle Charlie? No, no, no, no! Why not?"

Uncle Charlie sighed. "I can think of two reasons now. Later, several more will come to me. In the first place, you will be told that France needs you. No one has ever been able to resist such a suggestion, here or elsewhere. Let a man, old, sick, stupid, tired, cynical, wise, even dangerous to the future of his country, be told that his country needs him and him alone, and he will

respond even though he must be carried to the rostrum on a
stretcher and take the oath and Extreme Unction simultane-
ously. No, I can see no escape for you. If they tell you that
France needs you, you are lost. You can only pray that France
is not also lost."

"But maybe—"

"You see," said Uncle Charlie, "you are already caught. The
second force is more subtle but no less powerful. It is the over-
whelming numerical strength of the aristocracy. Let me develop
this.

"Aristocracy thrives and breeds most luxuriantly under democratic or republican regimes. Whereas in a kingdom the aristocrats are screened and controlled, even eliminated for one
reason or another, in republican climates the noblesse breed
like rabbits. At the same time, the lower orders seem to become
sterile. You will find the best proof of this in America, where
there is no single individual who is not descended from an aristocrat, where there is not even an Indian who is not a tribal
chief. In republican France, to only a slightly lesser degree, the
aristocracy has shown a fecundity beyond belief.

"They will be down on you like sparrows on a— No, I won't
complete that simile. They will demand privileges unremem-
bered since Louis the Ugly, but more than that, my dear child,
they will want money."

Pippin said miserably, "What am I to do, Uncle Charlie?
Why couldn't it have waited a generation or two? Isn't there a
collateral branch of the family who might—"

"No," said Charles, "there isn't. And if there were, the combination of reason number one, plus Madame, plus Clotilde,
would pull you under. And there's another thing. If every
Frenchman should oppose your accession to the monarchy,
every Frenchwoman would force you to reign. Too long have
they looked with craving eyes across the channel, sneered at the
frumpiness of British royalty, and envied it.

"Pippin, my child, you are sunk," said Charles. "You are the
royal patsy. I suggest that you search deeply in the situation for
something to enjoy. And now I know you will excuse me. A
client is coming in with three unsigned Renoirs."

Pippin said, "Well, anyway, I don't feel so alone, knowing that you will have to assume your titles."

"Name of a thrice-soiled name!" cried Uncle Charlie. "I had forgotten that!"

In a daze, Pippin left the gallery. He wandered blindly up-Seine on the Left Bank, past Notre-Dame, past warehouses, past wine storage, over bridges, past factories, and he did not look around until he came to Bercy.

During his long and slow peramble it is more than possible that his mind, like a rat in a laboratory maze, sought every possible avenue of escape, explored runways and aisles and holes, only to run against the wire netting of fact. Again and again he butted his mental nose against the screen at the end of a promising passage, and there was the fact. He was king and there was no escaping it.

In Bercy he stumbled wearily into a café, sat at a small marble table, observed, without seeing it, a passionate domino game, and, although it was not yet noon, he ordered a Pernod. He drank so rapidly and ordered another so promptly that the domino-players thought him a tourist and guarded their language.

With his third Pernod, Pippin was heard to say, "All right, then. All right, then." He swallowed his drink and waved for another and, when it came, he addressed his glass.

"So you want a king, my friends? But have you considered the danger? Do you know what you might have conjured up?" He turned to the domino-players. "Will you do me the honor of drinking a toast with me?" he demanded.

Sullenly they accepted. For an American, they thought, he spoke excellent French.

When they were served, Pippin raised his glass. "They want a king! I drink to the King! Long live the King!" He drained his glass. "Very well, my friends," he said. "It is just possible that they will *get* a king—and that's the last thing in the world they want. Yes, they may find they have a king on their hands." He got up from his table and moved to the door. It was noted that he had a slow and regal step.

It is not so easy as might appear on the surface to reactivate a monarchy. There is the matter of what kind of monarchy you are going to have. Pippin leaned strongly toward the constitutional form, not only because he was a liberal man at heart, but also because the responsibility of absolutism is very great. He owned himself too lazy to make all the effort for success and too cowardly to take all the blame for mistakes.

The meeting of all parties called to determine procedure constituted itself, at Pippin's request, a deliberative body. A troubling question was introduced by the king very early in the discussion.

What would the American government think of the change, and would the American State Department be likely to continue to recommend the same financial aid to the Kingdom as it had to the Republic of France?

M. Flosse, representing both Right and Left Centrists, was able to put any such doubts to rest. "It is the nature of American foreign policy to distrust liberal governments and strongly to favor the more authoritarian, which it considers the more responsible."

M. Flosse named Venezuela, Portugal, Saudi Arabia, Trans-Jordan, Egypt, Spain, and Monaco as examples of this American peculiarity. He went even further, proving that the People's Republics of the USSR, plus Poland, Czechoslovakia, Bulgaria, China, and North Korea, also had in the past shown a strong preference for dictatorships and absolute monarchies over democratically elected governments.

It was not necessary to inquire into the reasons for these preferences, said M. Flosse. Indeed, it might even be embarrassing. The fact that such preference was a historical fact was sufficient. In the case of America, he went on, there was, in addition, a sentimental attachment for the throne of France.

"When the American colonies were alone in their war for independence, who came to their aid with men, money, and material? A republic? No, the Kingdom of France. Who crossed the ocean to serve in the armies of America? Common people? No, aristocrats."

M. Flosse suggested that the king's first official act should be to request a subsidy for his government from America for the purpose of making France strong against Communism, and an equal subsidy from the Communist nations in the interests of world peace.

The enthusiastic response from both the United States and the Union of Soviet Socialist Republics is proof enough that M. Flosse had properly assessed the situation. It is history by now that not only did the American Congress advance more money than was requested, but also that the Lafayette Fund, collected from schoolchildren, made possible the beginning of the refurbishing of the royal quarters at Versailles.

After the first explosion of enthusiasm there was some worry among government functionaries: the postmen, the inspectors, the myriad of little officials, public toilet keepers, national monument guardians, custom inspectors, inspectors of inspectors, all of whom feared on second consideration that their livings might be curtailed. A general proclamation from the king, freezing the status quo, however, put all minds at rest and created a passionate loyalty among the concessionaires.

At this time the Minister of National Monuments presented a bill to the king for three hundred thousand francs, an expense incurred when the Princess Clotilde not only turned on the fountains at Versailles but also made use of the floodlights during two whole nights. The princess herself had waved the bill aside regally.

Pippin was able to prove that his total balance in the Chase Bank in the Rue Cambon was one hundred and twenty thousand francs. The first loan from America, however, solved the matter to everyone's satisfaction.

Complex as it was to establish the monarchy, the actual crowning of the king at Reims proved even more difficult. Charles had been correct in his estimate of the increase in the numbers of the aristocracy under the Republic. Not only had the noblesse multiplied beyond all belief, but they could not agree on the actual form of the crowning. That it should take an ancient and traditional form was conceded, but which ancient form?

Vitally interested groups demanded that the crowning be put off until the summer. The Couture was swamped with orders for court dresses. The ceramics industries needed time to make the millions of cups and plates and ashtrays and plaques bearing not only the royal arms, but the profile of the king and queen. The summer would bring a tidal wave of tourists, which alone would make the whole venture profitable.

Matters not previously contemplated became of vital importance. Newly appointed lords of protocol, kings-at-arms, nobles of the bedchamber, ladies in waiting ran in circles, while the offices of the Royal Historians were lighted all night.

The museums were ransacked for coaches, for costumes, for flags. The libraries were turned inside out. The coinage had to be changed. There was no artist whose brush and palette could not find employment in repainting coats of arms and armorial bearings. Such had been the progenitive activity of the nobility that every shield required new quarterings. By general agreement the bend sinister was abandoned, since its inclusion would have given a tiresome sameness to the bearings of the living and a lack of dignity to the hatchments of the deceased.

Carriage-makers, unemployed for half a lifetime, were dragged out of senile retirement to swell the spokes and felloes of state coaches and to direct the replacement of leather springs.

Armorers relearned the burnishing and lubrication of gauntlets, of greaves, of visors, of basinets, for many of the younger peers insisted on attending the coronation armed cap-a-pie, regardless of the weather.

The nylon industry put on an extra shift in all plants to fill the demand for velvets and artificial mothproof ermine.

The actual crown presented a problem, since it did not exist. However, Van Cleef and Arpels, Harry Winston, and Tiffany's pooled their resources, their craftsmen, and their precious stones to create a diadem three feet high and so thickly jeweled that a support had to be built on the back of the throne, else its weight would have broken the neck of the monarch. This crown was carried by four priests and when, after the coronation, it was broken up and its individual stones properly attested, it sold for a profit of twelve million dollars and the firms which had created it were granted the right to display the royal arms and to use the title "Crown Makers to the King of France."

Apart from affairs of state, of finance, of international relations, and of protocol, a change from republic to monarchy involved a thousand details which might escape the ordinary citizen.

In Paris schools sprang up to revivify lost arts and graces— Schools of the Walk (with or without staff), Schools of the Bow, of the Curtsy, the Hand Kiss; Schools of the Fan, Schools of the Insult, Schools of Honor. Fencing masters found their classes crowded. Old General Victor Gonzel, who is the world's final authority on the proper use of the muzzle-loading pistol, gave daily instructions to half a hundred budding courtiers.

On all of this preparation Pippin looked with consternation. A delegation proposing to establish a company of Life Guards armed with halberds made him miss an eclipse of the moon. The clamors of the Hereditary Royal Order of Dwarfs drove him to seclusion in the rear of Uncle Charles's gallery.

"The Folies Bergère is holding a competition," he complained. "They are choosing a King's Mistress. Uncle Charlie, in my young days when it was expected of me, I went along with our national practice even though it was expensive and, after a while, boring. But now—do you know they have entries from every nation in the world? I won't do it, Uncle Charlie. Even Marie has been after me about it. Damn it, Uncle Charlie, have you ever heard those girls talk?"

"I have by various methods sought to avoid that," said Uncle Charlie. "My child, in some things you may be able to assert your royal authority, but if you think you can be King of France without a mistress to enlighten your people with her extravagance and her charming unreliability, you are very much mistaken."

"But kings' mistresses have kept the nation in hot water almost invariably."

"Of course, my boy. Of course, that is part of it. Has your astronomy robbed you of any sense of proportion or knowledge of history?"

"I'll get myself a minister," said Pippin violently. "That's what I'll do! Somewhere I'll find myself a Mazarin or a Richelieu and let him do the work."

"You'll find that a minister worth his salt will be very firm about a mistress," said Uncle Charles. "Figure it to yourself— it would be like going without your clothes. The French nation would not tolerate it."

"I don't have any privacy," said Pippin. "I am not even crowned yet and already I haven't a moment of peace. And I must say you are not taking your hereditary duties very seriously. The report has come to me that you have uncovered a whole atticful of unsigned Bouchers."

"A man must live," said his uncle. "But you must not imagine that I have deserted you. I have been thinking on your behalf. Pippin, I want your complete attention. In America a chief executive who has found the duties and requirements of his office in conflict with his interests has discovered an interesting and practical expedient. He has turned over details of his office or of his party to one of the great advertising agencies.

"Now these companies, with their huge staffs and—how do you say it?—their 'know-how,' are able to manage public relations, organization, correspondence, news releases, and appointments. If such a company can merchandise a president and a political party, why not a king? Consider their intelligence! In foreign relations their policy derives not from some disinterested public servant, but from doing the most profitable business with the principality in question. And who would be more tender and wise than an agency whose profits depend on its tenderness and its wisdom? If such a connection could be made, Pippin, you could go back to your telescope. The advertising agency would handle everything and would also see that proper reports were furnished to the press. Why, they would even take care of the career of your mistress."

"It sounds ideal," said Pippin.

"Oh! There is more than that, my boy. Consider the simple matter of a speech on television. I can foresee that you will have to appear on television as King of France."

"What do they do?"

"Let us say the president must make a speech. Nothing is left to accident. He is rehearsed by an authority in speech, in pronunciation, and in emotion; coached by a man who has proved beyond doubt his—what they call 'draw.'"

"Like Marilyn Monroe—"

"Well, something like. But that is not all. He then is made up by the Westmore Brothers, the best. He does not just talk. Not at all. He has a stage manager, the scene is set. It is rehearsed. It rises to a glorious climax. If the man were simply speaking, he might *be* sincere, but he would not *sound* sincere, and this is important because the speaker did not write the speech, you see. The agency did. The duties of the office sometimes make it impossible for the president even to read the speech before he goes into rehearsal. I wonder—"

"What?"

"Do you have a dog?"

"Marie has a cat."

"Never mind. Maybe it is not so important in France."

"Do you think one of those agencies would take the account, Uncle Charlie?" Pippin demanded eagerly. "Would it be worth their while?"

"I shall make discreet inquiries, my child. At least it will do no harm to ask. Even if it were not as profitable as other accounts, a reputable agency might feel that the prestige of representing the King of France would be worth their while. It is called 'institutional prestige,' I believe. I shall inquire, Pippin. We can only hope."

"I do sincerely hope," said the king.

The spring in Paris was traditionally beautiful. Production of all things royal and all things French caused factories to put on night shifts. An era of good feeling and security justified a reduction in wages.

As might have been expected, Madame took the change in her status with realism and vigor. To her it was like moving from one apartment to another—on a larger scale, of course, but having the same problems. Madame made lists. She complained that her husband did not take his duties as seriously as he should.

"You loll about the house," she said to him, "when anyone can see that there are a thousand things to be done."

"I know," said Pippin in the tone she knew meant he had not listened.

"You just sit around reading."

"I know, my dear."

"What are you reading that is so important at a time like this?"

"I beg your pardon?"

"I said, what are you reading?"

"History."

"History? At a time like this?"

"I have been going over the history of my family and also the records of some of the families which followed us."

Madame said tartly, "It has always seemed to me that the Kings of France, with singularly few gifts, have done very well for themselves. There are some exceptions, of course."

"It is the exceptions I am thinking of, my dear. I have been thinking of the Sixteenth Louis. He was a good man. His intentions and his impulses were good."

"Perhaps he was a fool," said Marie.

"Perhaps he was," said Pippin. "But I understand him, even though we are not of the same family. To a certain extent I think I am like him. I am trying to see where he made his errors. I should hate to fall into the same trap."

"While you have been daydreaming, have you given a single thought to your daughter?"

"What has she done now?" Pippin demanded.

It cannot be denied that Clotilde had led a rather unusual existence. When, at fifteen, she wrote the best-selling novel *Adieu Ma Vie*, she was sought out and courted by the most celebrated and complex minds of our times. She was acclaimed by the Reductionists, the Resurrectionists, the Protonists, the Non-Existentialists, and the Quantumists, while the very nature of her book set hundreds of psychoanalysists clamoring to sift her unconscious. She had her table at the Café des Trois Puces, where she held court and freely answered questions on religion, philosophy, politics, and aesthetics. It was at this very table that she started her second novel, which, while never finished, was to be titled *Le Printemps des Mortes*. Her devotees formed the school called Clotildisme, which was denounced by the clergy and caused sixty-eight adolescents to commit ecstatic suicide by leaping from the top of the Arc de Triomphe.

Clotilde's subsequent involvement in politics and religion

was followed by her symbolic marriage to a white bull in the Bois de Boulogne. Her celebrated affairs of honor, in which she wounded three elderly Academicians and herself received a rapier thrust in the right buttock, caused some comment—and all this before she was twenty. In an article in *Souffrance,* she wrote that her career had left her no time for childhood.

She then reached the phase when she spent her afternoons at the movies and her evenings arguing the merits of Gregory Peck, Tab Hunter, Marlon Brando, and Frank Sinatra. Marilyn Monroe she found overbloomed and Lollobrigida bovine. She went to Rome, where she acted in three versions of *War and Peace* and two of *Quo Vadis,* but her notices threw her into such despair that her elevation to Princess Royale came just in time. In this field the competition was less fierce.

Clotilde began to think of herself, at least pronominally, in the plural. She referred to "our people," "our position," "our duty." Her first royal act, that of turning on the fountains at Versailles, was followed by a detailed plan very dear to her heart and not without its parallel in history. She set apart an area quite near to Versailles, to be called "Le Petit Round-Up." Here there would be small ranch houses, corrals, barns, bunkhouses. Here branding irons would be constantly in bon-fires and cayuses would leap wild-eyed against the barriers. To Le Petit Round-Up would come Roy Rogers, Alan Ladd, Hoot Gibson, Gary Cooper, the taciturn and the strong. They would feel at home at Le Petit Round-Up. Clotilde, in leather skirt and black shirt, would move about, serving red-eye in shot-glasses. If there were gun-play—and how can this be avoided where passionate and inarticulate men gather?—then the princess would be ready to stanch wounds and cool with her royal hand the pain-wracked but silent sufferer. This was only one of Clotilde's plans for the future.

It was at this time that she began to take her old Teddy bear to bed. It was at this time that she fell madly in love with Tod Johnson.

Clotilde met him at Les Ambassadeurs, where she had gone with young Georges de Marine—the Comte de Marine, that is, who was seventeen and listless. Georges knew perfectly well

that Clotilde knew Tab Hunter was in Paris. He knew also, because he belonged to the same fan club, that Tab Hunter would
put in an appearance at Les Ambassadeurs sometime during
the evening.

Tod Johnson sat next to Clotilde in the banquette seats
which faced the dance floor. She noticed him with a quickened
breath, watched him with blood-pounding interest, and finally,
under the roaring of violins, she leaned toward him and asked,
"You are American?"

"Sure."

"Then you must be careful. They will keep opening champagne if you do not tell them to stop."

"Thank you," said Tod. "They already have. You are
French?"

"Of course."

"I didn't think any French people came here," said Tod.

Georges kicked Clotilde viciously on the ankle, and her face
reddened with pain.

Tod said, "I hope you don't mind. May I introduce myself? I
am Tod Johnson."

"I know how you do these things in America," Clotilde said.
"I have been to America. May I introduce the Comte de Ma-
rine? Now," she said to Georges, "you must introduce me.
That is how they do it."

Georges squinted his eyes craftily. "Mademoiselle Clotilde
Héristal," he said evenly.

Tod said, "That name rings a bell. Are you an actress?"

Clotilde dropped her eyelashes. "No, Monsieur, except in so
far as everyone is an actress."

"That's good," said Tod. "Your English is wonderful."

Georges spoke without inflection in the tone he considered
insulting. "Does Monsieur perhaps speak French?"

"Princeton French," said Tod. "I can ask questions but I
can't understand the answers. But I'm learning. It isn't all running together the way it did a few weeks ago."

"You stay a while in Paris?"

"I don't have any plans. Would you permit me to order
champagne?"

"If you will tell them to stop. You must not let them cheat you as though you were some Argentine."

That is how it started.

Tod Johnson was the ideal American young man—tall, stiff-haired, blue-eyed, well dressed, well educated by going standards, well mannered, and soft-spoken. He was equally fortunate in his background. His father, H. W. Johnson, the Egg King of Petaluma, California, was reputed to have two hundred and thirty million white leghorn chickens. Even more fortunate was the fact that H. W. was a poor man who had built his chicken kingdom by his own efforts.

It will be seen that, although Tod Johnson was very rich, he did not suffer from lineage. At the end of his six months' shake-down in Europe he was expected to go home to Petaluma and begin at the bottom of the chicken business, eventually to rise to the top and take it over.

It was only after several meetings with Clotilde that he told her about his father and the egg empire. By then she was so warm and gooey with love that she forgot to tell him her own family news. Clotilde the novelist, the worldly, the Communist, the princess, had for the moment ceased to exist. At twenty she slopped into a fifteen-year-old love affair, all sighs and a full gassy feeling in the stomach. She was so vague and listless that Madame gave her an old country remedy that put her to bed in earnest and removed the necessity for a psychiatrist. Her body was so hard put to survive the remedy that her mind was left to take care of itself. When this happens the mind does very well. Her love remained, but she found she could breathe again.

19— was a monster year for American advertising. BBD & O was up to its ears rewriting the Constitution of the United States and at the same time marketing a new golf-mobile with pontoons.

Riker, Dunlap, Hodgson, and Fellows would have taken the French job in the fall, but could not pull its key people off promotion of Nudent, the dentrifice which grows teeth.

Merchison Associates was busy with a transatlantic pipeline, called in the public press "Tapal," a twenty-four-inch main which ran under the sea from Saudi Arabia to New Jersey with floating pumping stations every fifty miles. The matter would not have been so difficult but for the constant meddling of Senator Banger, Democrat, New Mexico, with his nuisance questioning as to why army and navy personnel and material were being used by a privately owned corporation. Merchison Associates were in Washington most of the spring and summer. If any of these agencies had been free to function, the coronation of the King of France might have been run more smoothly.

Who could set down all the drama, the pageantry and glories, and, yes, the confusion of the coronation at Reims on July 15? Newspaper coverage ran to many millions of words. Color photographs filled the split-page of every newspaper with a circulation of more than twenty thousand.

The New York *Daily News* front page carried a headline, of which each letter was four inches high, that read: FROGS CROWN PIP.

Every byline writer and commentator in America was in attendance.

Conrad Hilton took this occasion to open the Versailles-Hilton.

The life story of every aristocrat in France was bought in advance.

Louelle Parsons had a front-page box headed: WILL CLOTILDE COME TO HOLLYWOOD?

The reader should consult back issues of newspapers for accounts of the great day at Reims and Paris—the cathedral crowded to the doors, the cries of the scalpers, the stands of ceramics, the miniatures of royal coaches, the crush of people in the square, the traffic jam on the road to Reims, unparalleled even at the finish of the Tour de France. One company made a small fortune selling miniature guillotines.

The coronation itself was a triumph of disorder. It was dis-

covered at the last moment that horses had not been provided
to draw the state coaches, but this lack was filled by the abat-
toirs of Paris, even though their gesture made certain sections
of Paris meatless for three days. Miss France, representing Joan
of Arc, stood beside the throne, banner in one hand and drawn
sword in the other, until she fainted from heat and the weight
of her armor. She crashed with the sound of falling kitchenware
during the royal oath. However, six altarboys quickly propped
her against a Gothic column, where she remained forgotten until late in the evening.

The Communists, acting purely from habit, painted "Go
Home Napoleon" on the walls of the cathedral, but this slip
both in history and in manners was taken by all with good
humor.

The coronation was completed by eleven in the morning.
Then the wave of spectators rushed back to Paris for the parade which was to move from the Place de la Concorde to the
Arc de Triomphe. This state procession was scheduled for two
o'clock. It started at five.

The windows along the Champs Elysées were sold out. A
place at the curb brought as much as five thousand francs. The
owners of stepladders were able to extend their vacations in the
country by a week or more.

The procession was artfully arranged to represent past and
present. First came the state carriages of the Great Peers, deco-
rated with gold leaf and tumbling angels; then a battery of
heavy artillery drawn by tractors; then a company of crossbowmen in slashed doublets and plumed hats; then a regiment
of dragoons with burnished breastplates; then a group of heavy
tanks and weapon-carriers, followed by the Noble Youth in full
armor. A battalion of paratroopers followed, armed with submachine guns, leading the king's ministers in their robes of
office, and behind them a platoon of musketeers in lace, knee-
breeches, silk stockings, and high-heeled shoes with great buckles. These last moved along regally, using their musket crutches
as staffs.

At last the royal coach creaked by. Pippin IV, an uncomfortable bundle of purple velvet and ermine, with the queen,

48 JOHN STEINBECK

equally befurred, sitting beside him, acknowledged the cheers of the loyal bystanders and responded with equal courtesy to hisses.

Where the Avenue de Marigny crosses the Champs Elysées, a crazed critic fired a pistol at the king, using a periscope to aim over the heads of the crowd. He killed a royal horse. A musketeer of the Rear Guard gallantly cut it free and took its place in harness. The coach moved on.

For this loyal service the musketeer, Raoul de Potoir by name, demanded and received a pension for life.

The procession moved on: bands, ambassadors, professions, veterans, peasants in nylon country dress, leaders of parties, and loyal factions.

When at last the royal coach reached the Arc de Triomphe, the streets about the Place de la Concorde were still blocked with marchers waiting to get into the parade. But all of this is a matter of public record and of unparalleled newspaper coverage.

As the royal coach paused at the Arc de Triomphe, Queen Marie turned to speak to the king and found him gone. He had propped up his royal robes and crept away unnoticed in the crowd.

It was an angry queen who found him later, sitting on his balcony, polishing the eyepiece of his telescope.

"This is a fine thing," she said. "I have never been so embarrassed in my life. What will the papers say? You will be the laughingstock of the world. What will the English say? Oh, I know. They won't say anything, but they'll look, and you'll see in their eyes that they remember how *their* queen stood and sat, stood and sat for thirteen hours without even going to the— Pippin, will you stop polishing that silly glass?"

"Be silent," Pippin said softly.

"I beg your pardon?"

"You have it, my dear, but be silent."

"I don't understand you," cried Marie. "Where in the world do you find the right to tell me to be silent? Who do you think you are?"

"*I am the King,*" said Pippin, and this had not occurred to

Marie. "That's funny," he said. "I am, you know." And it was so obviously true that Marie looked at him with startled eyes.

"Yes, Sire," she said, and was silent.

"Starting to be a king is difficult, my dear," he said apologetically.

The king paced back and forth in Charles Martel's room.

"You don't answer the telephone," he complained. "You pay no attention to the pneumatique. I see there on the bust of Napoleon three letters delivered by hand, unopened. What is your explanation, sir?"

"Don't be so damn royal with me," said Uncle Charlie irritably. "I don't even dare go out on the street. I haven't taken my shutters down since the coronation."

"Which you did not attend," said the king.

"Which I did not dare attend. I am driven to despair. Descendants of the old nobility think I have your private ear. I am glad to be able to tell the truth—that I have not seen you. There is a line in front of my shop every day. Were you followed here?"

"Followed? I was escorted!" said the king. "I haven't been alone for a week. They watch me awaken. They help me dress. They are in my bedroom. They practically come into my bathroom. When I crack my eggs their lips tighten. When I raise my spoon their eyes follow it to my mouth. And you think you are driven—"

"But you are their property," said Uncle Charlie. "You, my dear nephew, are an extension of your people, and they have inalienable rights over your person."

"I can't imagine how I let myself in for this," said Pippin. "I didn't want to move to Versailles. I wasn't asked. I was moved. It's drafty there, Uncle Charlie. The beds are horrible. The floors creak. What are you mixing there?"

"A martini," said Uncle Charlie. "I've learned it from a young friend of Clotilde's, an American. The first taste is dreadful, but it becomes progressively more delicious. It has some of the hypnotic qualities of morphine. Try it! Don't let the ice frighten you."

"That's horrible," said the king and he drained the little glass. "Pour me another one, will you?" He licked his lips. "I had forgotten that the king has guests, built-in guests. Two hundred aristocrats are living with me at Versailles."

"Well, you have room for them."

"Room, yes, but nothing else. They sleep on the floor, in the halls. They've broken up the furniture to burn in the fireplaces to keep warm."

"In August?"

"Versailles would be cold in hell," said the king. "Say, what is in this? Gin I can taste, but what else?"

"Vermouth. Just a breath of vermouth. When they become delicious you've had too many. Try sipping this one, Sire. You are nervous, my child."

"Nervous? Why wouldn't I be nervous? Uncle Charlie, I am sure that somewhere in France there must be aristocrats who are solvent, but not among my guests. The word has gone out, under the bridges and under the barrows and to the subway gratings. I am surrounded by what, if they were not so high-born, would be called bums, but stately bums. They stroll majestically in the gardens. They touch their lips with bits of lace. They speak in words directly out of Corneille. And they aren't honest, Uncle Charlie. They steal."

"What do you mean, 'they steal'?"

"My uncle, there isn't a hen coop nor a rabbit hutch within ten miles that is safe from them. When the farmers complain, my guests smile and lash out the lace handkerchiefs they have shoplifted from Printemps. I have had complaints about that too. Every department store in Paris has set up a Nobility Detail to protect its counters. I'm afraid, Uncle Charlie; I am told the peasants are beginning to sharpen their scythes."

"Maybe you'll have to modernize the throne, my dear nephew; you may have to take a stand. You understand, of course, that what to ordinary people is simple theft, to the nobility is their ancient right. Do you think you ought to have another? Your color is a little high."

"What do you call them?"

"Martinis."

"Italian?"

"It isn't," said Uncle Charlie. "Pippin, I don't want you to leave me, but I think it only fair to warn you that Clotilde is bringing her new friend. I've opened the little rear door for my own convenience. If you would care to leave without being seen—"

"What friend is this?"

"An American friend. I thought he might be interested in some sketches."

"Uncle Charlie!"

"A man must live, my nephew. No royal revenues have been assigned to me. Are there any royal revenues, by the way?"

"Not that I know of," said the king. "There's the new American loan, but the Privy Council won't release any of it. You know the Privy Council is not unlike the recent republican government."

"Why shouldn't it be?" said Uncle Charlie. "It's the same people. As I said, the little rear door opens into the alley."

"Are you going to use your position to cheat this American? Uncle Charlie, is that the noble thing to do?"

"As a matter of fact, it is," said Charles Martel. "We invented it. I make no representations. If he likes a picture, he buys it. I simply say Boucher *might* have painted it. So he might. Anything is possible."

"But you are the king's uncle! To cheat a commoner, and an American commoner, at that, is—is like shooting sitting birds. The British would take a dim view of it."

"The British have developed their own methods of combining aristocracy with profit. They have more recent experience than we. But we will learn—and meanwhile, what is wrong with practicing on a rich American?"

"He is rich?"

"He is what the Americans call 'loaded.' His father is the Egg King of a province called Petaluma."

"Well, at least you're not stealing from the—the lower orders."

"Indeed I am not, my child. In America one only becomes a member of the lower orders when one is insolvent."

"Uncle Charlie, if you're making another one of those what-do-you-call-thems, I think I will stay and meet this Egg Prince. Is Clotilde serious in this—friendship?"

"I should hope so," said Uncle Charlie. "His father, H. W. Johnson, the king, has two hundred and thirty million chickens."

"Gracious!" said Pippin. "Well, thank Heaven Clotilde is not falling into the error of a certain English princess, giving her heart to a commoner. Thank you, Uncle Charlie. You know, you're getting the knack. This is far superior to the first one."

Tod Johnson was no more born to the purple than was the original Charles Martel. In 1932 the Johnson Grocery in Petaluma, California, nudged on by what was called "The Great Depression," slipped quietly out of existence. In 1933 H. W. Johnson, Tod's father, was enrolled on federal relief and assigned to roadwork.

H. W. Johnson never blamed President Hoover for the loss of his grocery store, but he could never forgive President Roosevelt for having fed him.

When, lacking refrigeration, the relief organization distributed live chickens, Mr. Johnson kept them a while before he ate them. He was fascinated by birds so unintelligent, which nevertheless could find subsistence in the weed patch behind his house.

During his two years on the road gang, Hank Johnson thought about chickens. When his grandmother died, leaving him three thousand dollars, he promptly bought ten thousand baby chicks. Most of this first venture died of a disease which darkened their combs and withered their feathers, but Johnson was not one to cry failure. It was hard enough to engage his interest in the first place, but once engaged, it was even more difficult to budge it. He wrote to the Department of Agriculture for its chicken booklet and from it he learned chicken economy.

Apart from diseases, he read, chickens are a luxury until you have fifty thousand of them. With that number, you may break even. With one hundred thousand you can show a small profit. Over half a million, you begin to get someplace.

One need not go into Mr. Johnson's organizational plans. They involved small investments by some of his neighbors and all of his relatives, who were persuaded to put up the capital for the intial two hundred thousand baby chicks. When half a million birds guaranteed a profit, this money was returned with thanks and a small bonus. From then on, H. W. Johnson was on his own.

Tod was three when the first million chicks marched in their little wire-floored cells. H. W. by that time was getting government surplus for feed and was selling eggs and fryers to the army and navy.

Tod went to the Petaluma public schools. In high school he joined the 4-H Club, where he learned a good deal about chickens: their habits, their diseases, and their propensities. He learned also to detest them for their stupidity, their odor, and their mess.

By the time he had graduated from high school there was no need for his further interest in the birds that were building the family fortune. H. W. Johnson was a factory by then. Dressed pullets and millions of eggs rolled off an assembly line. The Johnson offices were far from the smell and sight of chickens. The Johnson estate was on a lovely hill beyond the country club, while the Johnson energy and genius now concerned itself with figures rather than white leghorns. The unit was no longer a hen, but fifty thousand hens. The company had become a corporation with stock held by H. W. Johnson, Mrs. H. W. Johnson, Tod Johnson, and young Miss Hazel Johnson, a beautiful girl who on three separate occasions was named Egg Queen at the Petaluma Poultry Pageant.

It was now time for the family to expand to a dynasty, in the American pattern.

When Tod went to Princeton there were one hundred million chickens represented by stock certificates. But it must not be thought that only chickens were represented. Johnson, Inc., also sold feed, wire, brooders, incubators, refrigeration plants, and all the equipment which must be purchased by a small operator before he can proceed toward bankruptcy.

H. W. Johnson wore his title of Egg King gracefully and, true tycoon that he was, bought back his old grocery store and set it up as a museum. His only violence lay in his hatred for the Democratic party, for which he had every reason. Otherwise, he was a kindly, generous man, a man of vision. He had peacocks on his lawn at Johnson Vista and an artificial pond for white ducks.

Tod, meanwhile, dipped into four universities—Princeton for clothes, Harvard for accent, Yale for attitude, and the University of Virginia for manners. He emerged equipped for life with everything except the arts and foreign travel. The first he acquired in New York, where his taste for progressive jazz was developed, and his Grand Tour during the restoration of the French monarchy took care of the second.

His friendship with Clotilde grew like a mushroom in the caves of Paris, flourished like the pelargoniums in the flower boxes of the sidewalk cafés. Clotilde nurtured the pale plant with care, never letting it stray beyond Fouquet's on one side and the Hotel George V on the other, in which district Tod's Brooks-Brothers look did not cause comment. Neither would the princess be embarrassed by meeting any French people.

The affair reached its crescendo of passion, however, at the Select, when Tod leaned over the table, tore his eyes upward from her bosom, and said hoarsely, "Baby, you're a dish. A real dish."

Clotilde felt it to be a declaration. Afterward, inspecting her well-filled body in a full-length mirror, she growled, "I am a deesh."

Clotilde introduced her new friend to Uncle Charlie as a prospective husband, and Charlie accepted him as a prospective customer.

"You might be interested," he said to Tod, "in a group of paintings I have heard about. They have just come to light. Buried during the Occupation—"

"Uncle—please!" said Clotilde.

"I don't know much about painting, sir," said Tod.

"Perhaps you will learn," said Charles Martel happily, and later, after he had telephoned the Chase Bank, Paris Branch, he said to Clotilde, "I like that young man. He has an air. You must bring him again to call on me."

"Promise me you will not sell him pictures," the princess pleaded.

"My dear," said her great-uncle, "I have made certain discreet inquiries. Should I rob this young man of beauty and art simply because he is rich? Figure to yourself how many are two hundred and thirty million chicks. If one took twenty centimeters as the approximate length of one chicken, they would be—let me see—forty-six million meters, which is forty-six thousand kilometers, which is a procession of chickens extending nearly twice around the world at the equator—imagine!"

"What would they be going around the world for?" Clotilde asked.

"I beg your pardon?" said Uncle Charlie. "Oh! Please ask your friend to show me again how to make those—those martinis. There is something I do not accomplish."

Clotilde was surprised to find her father in the back room of the Galerie Martel, but she said, "Sire, I wish to present Mr. Tod Johnson. Mr. Tod Johnson, this is my father"—she blushed—"the king."

"Glad to know you, Mr. King," said Tod.

Uncle Charlie said delicately, "Not Mister—*the*."

"Come again?" said Tod.

"Il n'est pas Monsieur King II est *Le Roi*."

"No kidding!" said Tod.

"He is very democratic," said Uncle Charlie.

"I voted the Democratic ticket," said Tod. "My old—my father would kill me if he knew. He's a Taft man."

Pippin spoke for the first time. "Correct me if I am wrong. Have I not heard that Monsieur Taft is dead?"

"That doesn't mean a thing to my father," said Tod. "Let's get this straight in my mind. What kind of a king?"

Pippin said, "I do not understand."

"I mean like—well, they call my father the Egg King, and Benny Goodman is the King of Swing, and like that."

Pippin cried, "You know Benny Goodman?"

"Well, not really, but I've sat close enough to his clarinet to get my ear splashed."

"What joy," said the king. "I have the recording from Carnegie Hall."

"I'm more on the progressive kick myself," said Tod.

"And you are right in a way," said Pippin. "This is creative and good, but you must allow, Monsieur Egg, that Goodman, he is classic—at least when he inserts himself in the groove."

"Say," said Tod, "you talk good for a—"

Pippin chuckled. "Were you about to say 'king' or 'Frog'?"

"How about that?" said Tod. "You aren't kidding me, sir?"

"I am King of France," said the king. "It was not my choice of profession."

"The hell you are!"

"The hell I'm not."

"How'd you learn talk like that, sir?"

"For a number of years I have subscribed to *Downbeat*," said Pippin.

"Well, that explains it." Tod turned to Clotilde. "Baby, I'm ape about him. He's a Georgier George."

Uncle Charlie cleared his throat. "Perhaps Monsieur Tod would care to see some of the paintings I spoke about. Apparently they were hidden during the Occupation of France. Two of them are attributed to Boucher."

"What do you mean, attributed?" Tod asked. "Aren't they signed?"

"Well, no. But there are many indications—the colors, the brush technique—"

"I'll lay it on the line, sir," Tod said. "I thought of buying a present for my father. You see, I want to stay away from the business a little longer and I'll have to put the bite on him. I thought a real nice present might grease the slide—not that it will fool him. He'll know what I'm up to, but he may go along with it. He doesn't mind being fooled if he knows about it."

"These paintings—" Uncle Charlie began.

"You say Boucher. I halfway remember him from Art Appreciation. Suppose I buy a Boucher with no signature. Know what will happen? Father will get an expert—he's hell on experts. And suppose this Boucher is a phony. You see the position I'd be in—hustling my own father."

"But a signature would save you that difficulty?"

"It would help. Understand, it wouldn't be certain. My father is no dope."

"Perhaps we had better look at something else," said Uncle Charlie. "I know where I can put my hand on a very nice Matisse *with* a signature. There is a 'Tête de Femme' of Rouault, very fine—or maybe you would like to see a veritable swarm of Pasquins. These will have a great future value."

"I'd like to look at everything," said Tod. "Bugsy said you were doing something wrong with the martinis."

"They do not taste the same."

"Are you getting them cold enough? Mac Kriendler once told me that the only good martini is a cold martini. Here, let me mix you one. Will you have one too, sir?"

"Thank you. I should like to discuss with you your father, the king."

"Egg King."

"Exactly. Has he been this for a long time?"

"Since the depression. He hit bottom then. That was before I was born."

"Then he invented his kingdom as he went along?"

"You might say that, sir. And in his line there is nobody who can touch him."

"He has a principality, your father?"

"Well, it's a corporation—kind of the same thing if you control the stock."

"My young friend, I hope you will come to see me very soon. I wish to discuss the king business with you."

"Where do you live, sir? Bugsy wouldn't ever tell me. I thought she was ashamed."

"Perhaps she was," said the king. "I live at the Palace at Versailles."

"Holy mackerel!" said Tod. "Wait till my old man hears this—"

As though in celebration of the king's return, the summer slipped benignly over France—warm, but not hot; cool, but not cold.

The rains waited until the flowers of the vines exchanged their pollen and set their clusters densely, and then gentle moisture stirred the growth. The earth gave sugar and the warm air breed. Before a single grape ripened, it was felt that, barring some ugly trick by nature, this would be a vintage year, the kind remembered from the time when an old man was young.

And the wheat headed full and yellow. The butter took an unearthly sweetness from the vintage grass. The truffles crowded

one another under the ground. The geese happily stuffed themselves until their livers nearly burst. The farmers complained, as
their duty demanded, but even their complaints had a cheerful
tone.

From overseas the tourists boiled in and every one of them
was rich and appreciative so that the porters were seen to
smile—whether you believe it or not. Taxi drivers scowled in a
good-humored way, and one or two were heard to say that perhaps ruin would not come this year, an admission they will not
care to have repeated.

And what of the political groups now firmly rooted in the Privy
Council? Even they had an era of good feeling. Christian Christians saw the churches full. Christian Atheists saw them empty.

The Socialists went happily about writing their own constitution for France.

The Communists were very busy explaining to one another a
shift in the party line which seemed to place leadership in the
hands of the people, a subtlety later to be explained and exploited. Besides this, the collective leadership in the Kremlin
not only had congratulated the French Crown but had offered
a tremendous loan.

Alexis Kroupoff, writing in *Pravda,* proved beyond question
that Lenin had foreseen this move on the part of the French and
had approved of it as a step in the direction of eventual socializa-
tion. This explanation put the French Communists under an ob-
ligation not only to tolerate but actually to support the monarchy.

The Non-Tax-Payers' League was lulled to a state of bliss,
since American and Russian loans made it unnecessary to collect any taxes at all. A few pessimists argued that there would
come a day of reckoning, but these were laughed to scorn as
prophets of gloom and pilloried by caricatures in nearly all the
French press.

The French Rotary Club grew to such proportions that it
achieved the strength and influence of a party itself.

The landlords prepared their plan for government subsidy in
addition to a rise in rent ceilings.

Right and Left Centrists were so confident of the future that they freely suggested a rise in prices together with a lowering of wages, and no riots ensued, which proved to most people that the Communists had indeed been defanged.

To such a stable government there was no end to the loans America was happy to advance. The outpouring of American money had the effect of strengthening the Royalist parties of Portugal, Spain, and Italy.

England looked dourly on.

At Versailles the nobility happily quarreled over an honors list of four thousand names while a secret committee went forward with plans for restoring the land of France to its ancient and obviously its proper owners.

As Marie was one of the first to point out, it was the king this and the king that . . . No one will ever know what the queen went through. Being a queen takes some doing, but you are never going to make a man understand this. Marie had ladies in waiting, certainly, but just ask a lady in waiting to do something and see where you get. And it wasn't as though there were nearly enough servants and what there were were public servants who would argue for an hour rather than turn a dust cloth and then complain to the privy councilor who had procured the appointment.

Consider, for a moment, that gigantic old dustbox Versailles. How could any human being keep it clean? The halls and staircases and chandeliers and corners and wainscoting seemed to draw dust. There had never been any plumbing worth mentioning inside the place, although there were millions of pipes to the fountains and the fish ponds outside.

The kitchens were miles away from the apartments, and just try to get a modern servant to carry a covered tray from the kitchens to the royal apartments. The king could not eat his meals in the state dining rooms. If he did he would have two hundred dinner guests, and the royal family were just managing to scrape by as it was. In dividing the royal monies nobody gave a thought to the queen. She ran from morning until night, and still the housekeeping kept ahead of her. The extravagance was enough to drive a good Frenchwoman insane.

Besides all this, there were the nobles in residence. Their bowings and scrapings and grand manners disgusted Marie. They were always deferring to her opinion and then not listening, particularly when she asked them—asked them nicely, mind you—please to turn out the lights when they left a room, please to pick up their dirty clothes, please to clean the bathtub after themselves. But it was worse than that. They ignored her requests that they stop breaking up the furniture to burn in the fireplaces, stop emptying their chamber pots in the garden. It was impossible for Marie to figure to herself how such people could live with themselves.

And would the king listen? King indeed! He had his head in the clouds even more than he had when he played at being an astronomer.

Clotilde was no help to her. Clotilde was in love, not in love like a well-brought-up French girl, but in slob-love like an American student at the Sorbonne. And Clotilde had gotten so grand or so forgetful that she no longer made her bed or even washed out her underthings.

Worst of all, Marie had no one to talk to, to complain to, to gossip with.

There is no doubt that every woman needs another woman now and then as an escape valve for the pressures of being a woman. For her the man's releases are not available, the killing of small or large animals, vicarious murder from a seat at the prize ring. Flight into the hidden kingdom of the abstract is denied her. The Church and the confessor can let out some of the tensions, but even that is sometimes not enough.

Marie needed the sanctuary of another woman. Her good sense revolted against the ladies in waiting and the intolerable corps of nobles. Being queen, she was fearful of old friends of her Marigny days, because they could not fail to use their fancied influence in the interest of their husbands.

Queen Marie, casting in her mind, thought of her old friend and schoolmate Suzanne Lescault.

———

Sister Hyacinthe was perfect as a companion to the queen. Her order was able to change a rule and to uncloister the nun upon recognition of certain advantages which might accrue to itself as well as the natural satisfaction of knowing that the dear queen was in good hands. Sister Hyacinthe was removed to Versailles and encelled in a lovely little room overlooking box hedges and a carp pool—a few steps, indeed, from the royal apartments.

It may never be known exactly how much Sister Hyacinthe contributed to the peace and security of France. For example:

The queen closed the door firmly, put her fists on her hips, and breathed so tightly that her nostrils whitened. "Suzanne, I'm not going to put up with that dirty Duchess of P—— another minute—the insulting, insufferable slut. Do you know what she said to me?"

"Gently, Marie," said Sister Hyacinthe. "Gently, my dear."

"What do you mean gently? I don't have to suffer—"

"Of course not, dear. Hand me a cigarette, will you?"

"What am I going to do?" the queen cried.

Sister Hyacinthe slipped a hairpin around the cigarette to keep stain from her fingers, and she blew the smoke from lips pursed to whistle. "Ask the duchess if she ever hears from Gogi!"

"Who?"

"Gogi," said Sister Hyacinthe. "He was a high-wire man, very handsome, but nervous. So many artists are."

"Ha!" said Marie, "I understand. I'll do it! Then we'll see what she does with her lifted face."

"You mean those scars, dear? No. Her face was not lifted. It was, you might say, dropped. Gogi was very nervous."

Marie charged for the door, her eyes shining. Under her breath, as she searched the long painted halls, she muttered, "My dear Duchess—have you heard from Gogi lately?"

Or again:

"Suzanne, the king is being a bore about this mistress business. The Privy Council has appealed to me. Do you think you could talk to the king about it?"

"I have just the mistress for him," said Sister Hyacinthe.

"Grand-niece of our Superior—quiet, well-bred, a little stocky, but, Marie, she does beautiful needlework. She could be valuable to you."

"He won't consider her. He won't even discuss it."

"He won't have to see her," said Sister Hyacinthe. "In fact, it might be better if he didn't."

Or again:

"I don't know what I'm going to do with Clotilde. She's sloppy and listless. She won't pick up her clothes. She's selfish and inattentive."

"We have this problem in the order sometimes, dear, particularly with young girls who confuse other impulses with the religious."

"And what do you do?"

"Walk calmly up to her and punch her in the nose."

"What good will that do?"

"It will get her attention," said Sister Hyacinthe.

The queen never regretted calling in her old friend. And in the palace the wayward nobility began to be nervously aware of a force, of an iron influence which could be neither ignored nor sneered out of existence.

For her birthday, Marie presented Sister Hyacinthe with a daily foot massage by the best man in Paris. She ordered a tall screen with two holes near the bottom, through which Suzanne's feet and ankles could protrude.

"I don't know what I would do without her," said the queen.

"What?" the king asked.

Pippin was in a state of shock for a long time. He said to himself in wonder and in fear, "I am the king and I don't even know what a king is." He read the stories of his ancestors. "But they wanted to be kings," he told himself. "At least most of them did. And some of them wanted to be more. There I have it. If I could only find some sense of mission, of divinity of purpose."

He visited his uncle again. "Am I right in thinking that you would be glad if you were not related to me?" he asked.

Uncle Charlie said, "You take it too hard."

"That's easy to say."

"I know. And I'm sorry I said it. I am your loyal subject."

"Well, suppose there were a revolt?"

"Do you want truth or loyalty?"

"I don't know—both, I guess."

Uncle Charlie said, "I will not hide from you that my position as your uncle has increased my business. I am doing very well, particularly with the tourists."

"Then your loyalty is tied to profit. Would you be disloyal if you suffered a loss?"

Uncle Charlie went behind a screen and brought out a bottle of cognac. "With water?" he asked.

"How good is the cognac?"

"I suggest water. . . . Now. You want to turn over stones and find the insects underneath. One always hopes for virtue—right up to the point of exercising it. I hope I would stick with you to the death. But I also hope that I would have the judgment to join the opposition a few moments before it is generally apparent that it will succeed."

"You are very honest, my uncle."

"Can you tell me what is really troubling you?"

Pippin sipped his fine à l'eau. He said uncertainly, "The function of a king is to rule. To rule, one must have power. To have power one must take power . . ."

"Go on, child."

"The men who forced the crown on me were not intent on giving anything away."

"Ah! You learn, I see. You are becoming what is called cynical by those who fear reality. And you feel that you are a wheel unturning, a plant without a flower."

"Something like that. A king without power is a contradiction in terms, and a king with power is an abomination."

"Excuse me," said Uncle Charlie. "Mice are moving on the cheese." He went to the front of his shop. "Yes?" Pippin heard him say. "It is lovely. If I told you who I suspect painted it— No. I must say I do not know. Notice the brushwork here, see how the composition soars—and the subject, the costume—

Oh! That? A nothing. Came in with a pile of trash from the cellar of a château. I haven't inspected it. I suppose you *could* buy it, but would it be wise? I would have to ask two hundred thousand francs because it would cost me that to have it cleaned and inspected. Consider again! Here, for example, is a Rouault about which there is no doubt . . ." There was a time of soft muttering, and then Uncle Charlie's voice. "Won't you let me dust it? I tell you I have not even inspected it."

In a few moments he came back, rubbing his hands.

"I'm ashamed of you," said the king.

Charles Martel went to a pile of dirty unframed canvases in a corner. "I must replace it," he said. "I do my best to discourage them. Perhaps I would feel worse if I did not know they thought they were cheating me." He carried the dusty painting to the front. "Ah, come in, Clotilde," he said. "Your father is here." He called, "It's Clotilde and the Egg Prince."

The three of them came past the red velvet drapery which hung over the doorway, and their passage left a thin cloud of dust in the air.

"Good evening, sir," said Tod. "He's teaching me the business. We're going to open galleries in Dallas and Cincinnati and one in Beverly Hills."

"Shame on him!" said the king.

"I try to discourage them but they demand—" Uncle Charlie began.

"Very clever," said the king. "But who tricks them into demanding?"

"I don't think that's quite fair, sir," said Tod. "The first function of business is to create the demand and the second to fulfill it. Think of all the things that wouldn't be made at all if people hadn't been told they needed them—medicines and cosmetics and deodorants. Can you say, sir, that the automobile is wasteful and unnecessary—that it keeps people in debt for transportation they don't need? You can't say that to people who want automobiles even if they and you know it is true."

"The line must be drawn somewhere," Pippin said. "Has my fine uncle told you why the Mona Lisa was stolen?"

"Now wait, dear nephew!"

Pippin cried, "He usually starts it—'I can't mention any names but I have heard'—Heard indeed!"

"It never made any sense to me," Tod said. "The Mona Lisa was stolen from the Louvre. Right? And then, after a year, it was returned. Do you mean they returned a fake?"

"Not at all," said the king. "The picture in the Louvre is genuine."

Clotilde pouted. "Must we talk business?"

"Wait, Bugsy, I want to hear."

"Go on, my uncle," said the king. "It's your story. It's your—"

"I can't say I approved of it," said Charles Martel, "and yet no honest person was injured."

Clotilde said, "Oh, tell him and get it over with."

"Well, I can't mention any names but I have heard that during the time the Mona Lisa was—away, eight Mona Lisas were bought by very rich men."

"Where?"

"Well, wherever very rich men were—Brazil, Argentina, Texas, New York, Hollywood . . ."

"But why was the original returned?"

"Well you see, once the picture was returned, there was no further search for the—ah—thief."

"Ah!" said Tod. "But how about the people who bought the fakes?"

Uncle Charlie said piously, "When you buy a stolen masterpiece, you are committing a crime. But even though they must hide the treasure, there do seem to be men capable of this. If, after they have bought, they discover the treasure to be a, shall we say, replica, these men are still not likely to discuss it. There are, I am told, rich men who are willing to be dishonest. I believe I am safe in saying there are none who are willing to admit they are fools."

Tod laughed. "So if they had been honest—"

"Exactly," said Uncle Charlie.

"Then why is the king against it?"

"He is sensitive."

Tod turned toward the king.

Pippin said slowly, "I believe that all men are honest where they are disinterested. I believe that most people are vulnerable where they are interested. I believe that some men are honest in spite of interest. It seems to me reprehensible to search out areas of weakness and to exploit them."

"Aren't you going to have some difficulty being king, sir?" Tod asked.

"He is already," Clotilde said bitterly. "He not only wants to be above everything, every human weakness, he wants his family to be too. He wants everybody to be good—and people just aren't good."

Pippin said, "Stop there, miss! I will not have you say that. People are good—just as long as they can be. Everybody wants to be good. That is why I resent it when goodness is made difficult or impossible for them."

Uncle Charlie said vindictively, "Before they came in, you were talking about power. You were saying, I believe, that a king without power is emasculate. If that is so, my dear nephew, what do you think of the proposition that power corrupts and absolute power corrupts absolutely?"

The king said, "Power does not corrupt. Fear corrupts, perhaps fear of a loss of power."

"But does not power create in other men the impulse which must cause fear in the holder of power? Can power exist without the ultimate fear that makes corruption? Can you have one without the other?"

"Oh, dear!" said Pippin. "I wish I knew."

Uncle Charlie bored in. "If you took power, don't you think the very people who made you king would turn against you?"

The king threw up his hands, "And you told me to relax! To you these things are only ideas. To me—I eat them and dress in them, breathe them and dream of them. Uncle Charlie, this is no intellectual game to me. It is anguish."

"My poor child," said Uncle Charlie. "I did not mean to hurt you. Wait! I will get another bottle. This time you shall have it without water."

Tod watched the king sip his brandy and ruddy relaxation come over him. The tremble went out of his hands and lips and he loosened his muscles to the embrace of the velvet chair.

"Thank you," he said to Uncle Charlie. "This is exquisite cognac."

"It should be. It has been waiting around since the Treaty of Ghent. Will you have a little more? You will notice I have not offered it to these commoners."

Tod Johnson picked Clotilde's hand from her lap and held it between both of his.

"I've been worried, sir," he began uneasily. "You know I've been dating your daughter. I like her. Under ordinary circumstances, I wouldn't give a—I mean I'd just go ahead—but, you see, sir, I like you too, and, well—I want to ask you—"

Pippin smiled at him. "Thank you," he said. "I guess one of the hard things about being king is that no one can afford to like the king, nor can the king dare to like anyone. You are worried because Clotilde is a royal princess, is that not so?"

"Well, yes, and you know all the trouble they have had in England. I don't want to hurt her and, well—I'm—I don't want to get hurt myself."

Clotilde broke in angrily. "Toddy, is it that you place yourself to absorb a powder?"

"I don't think I understand," said Pippin. "What is this powder?"

Tod laughed. "Clotilde is taking a Berlitz course in American slang. I think her instructors are a little confused about it too. She means am I winding up for a run-out."

"Preparing to say adieu," Uncle Charlie filled in.

The king asked kindly, "And are you?"

"That's what I don't know. Now what I want to ask you is this: I've been reading a little. The French kings have always observed the Salic Law, is that not so? And this law says that women cannot succeed. Isn't that true also? And therefore it is not so important to the state who noblewomen marry? Is that so?"

Pippin nodded approvingly. "You have read properly. That is true up to a point. But in one place you are in error, and this has nothing to do with the Salic Law. Women of great houses have always been used as magnets for other great houses, along with their lands and their holdings and their titles."

"Kind of catalysts for mergers," Tod suggested.

Uncle Charlie broke in. "The Salic Law is not a law. It is only a custom brought to us by Germans. Don't give it a thought."

Pippin said, "My uncle, by your definition our ancestors were Germans too—Héristal, Arnulf." He turned back to Tod. "My young friend, I don't know what the decision will be about succession. Clotilde is my only child. I am not prepared to divorce my wife for the sake of an heir, and my wife has passed— But you understand. It is quite possible that public pressure may force Clotilde to be a breeding ground for kings. Custom, particularly meaningless custom, is generally more powerful than law. Would you be content to leave the—the powder untaken until we see? By the way, does this refer to gunpowder, or to medicinal powder?"

"Darned if I know," said Tod. "The only people who try to find out what slang means are the ones who can't use it. You mean, sir, that I should stick around a while?"

"Exactly," said the king. "You see, a second function of nice-looking noblewomen was to bring money into the family."

"If you're thinking of Petaluma, forget it," said Tod. "If I know my father, he'll have it tied up in trust funds and things."

"But you see," said Uncle Charlie, "his reputation for having it will make you not an undesirable suitor. The French resent more than anything else being fools. Marrying a rich man, no matter what the drawbacks, has never been considered foolish in France."

"I see. You're covering for me. Thanks. Make me kind of like part of the family—for a while, at least. That's why I asked in the first place. I know you're the king and you're older than I am but you haven't had much practice kinging. You've got a great little thing here, great, but it can blow up in your face if you don't play your cards right."

"This has happened in the past," said Pippin. "And not so very long ago either."

"I'd like to talk to you about that, sir, now that I'm a—you might say apprentice—member of the family."

Clotilde cried, "Nots! Politics. You are a droopys. I am a bore."

Tod laughed shortly. "Maybe she's right," he said. "They say that Americans talk sex in the office and business in the bedroom. I'll take her out violin-dodging, but I would like to talk to you."

"I should be glad," said Pippin. "Will you come to Versailles?"

"I've been out there," said Tod. "It's crawling with freeloaders. Tell you what, sir. Why don't you come to my suite at the George Cinq?"

The king said, "One of the drawbacks of my office is that I can't go where I wish. The management would have to be told, the secret police, the newspapers privately informed. Your suite would be searched and men placed on the roofs across the way. It's not very much fun to be royalty."

Tod said, "Not at the George Cinq. There hasn't been a Frenchman there in years. Besides, Ava Gardner and H. R. H. Kelly are in residence. You couldn't raise an eyebrow. It might be the most private place in France for a French king."

"Perhaps so," said Pippin. "I have even thought of disguises."

"My God," Uncle Charlie said, "you'd be so bad at it. You have absolutely no talent as an actor."

The queen drew her chair close to the chaise longue where Sister Hyacinthe sat in pious contemplation.

"I've always told you Pippin was vague," she said. "He was bad enough with his telescope, but he's worse now. He paces—with his hands behind his back—and he mutters. When I speak to him, he doesn't hear. And he is miserably unhappy. There's something on his mind. I wish you'd talk to him, Suzanne. You were always good with men—they say."

"They say," Sister Hyacinthe observed. "But maybe not good enough. What would I say to him?"

"Find out what's bothering him—"

"Maybe just being king is bothering him."

"Nonsense," said Marie. "Anybody would want to be king."

Marie steered her husband to Sister Hyacinthe's cell. "This is my old friend," she said, and then cleverly, "Oh! There's something I forgot. Excuse me for a moment." And she went out.

The king looked casually at the nun.

"Sit down, Sire."

"I haven't been very dutiful toward the Church. Since I was a child," he said.

"You might say I haven't either. I was twenty years on the musical stage."

"I thought you were familiar."

"In this costume? I am complimented, M'sieur. Very few ever looked at my face."

He tried for gallantry. "Then there must be incredible beauties . . ."

"Under this habit? Thank you. I went to school with Madame. You may have heard her speak of me as Mademoiselle Lescault. I don't think she will have mentioned my profession. Marie is one of those fortunate people who forbid existence to matters they do not approve of. I envy her this gift."

"My wife is remarkable in many ways, but not in subtlety. It is true that quite often I do not know what she is up to but I have never any doubt when she is up to something."

Suzanne put her head back and closed her eyes. "You wonder why she brought you here and left you here?"

"I imagine that is what I wonder."

"She feels that you are uneasy, restless."

"I have often been uneasy and nearly always restless. This has not troubled her before. She attacked it with sauces and small delicious sweets."

"That is the housewife's remedy. I hope it cured you, or at least that you said it did."

"I hope I tried, Sister."

"You are amiable, M'sieur. Could you tell me why you are uneasy now? Something I can twist around for Marie? She worries about you."

The king said, "I would help you if I could. Many of the causes I do not know myself. I did not ask to be king. I was picked like a berry from a bush and placed in a position where there are many precedents, nearly all of them bad and all of them successful."

"You cannot, like a berry, let happen what will happen?"

"No," said the king, "it is the misfortune of men to want to do a thing well, even a thing they do not want to do at all. You will not believe this, Sister, but once I wanted to dance well. It was ridiculous."

"You are afraid you will make mistakes?"

"My dear Sister, the path is solid with mistakes. Even the best of kings failed."

"I am sorry for you."

"No, you must not be sorry. My uncle told me I had the choice of cutting my wrists. I did not take advantage of it."

Sister Hyacinthe said, "There have been kings who put the whole business in others' hands—the ministry, the council, the team—and went about enjoying themselves."

"I think, Sister, that was only after they had given up. There is a strong pressure on a king to be a king. The purpose of a king is to rule and the purpose of rule is to increase the well-being of the kingdom."

"It is a trap," said Sister Hyacinthe, "like all other virtue—it is a trap. Where virtue is involved it is very difficult to tell one-self the truth, M'sieur. There are two kinds of virtue. One is passionate ambition and the other simply a desire for the peace which comes from not giving anyone any trouble."

"You are thoughtful, Sister," said the king, and she knew from the brightness of his eyes that she had captured his attention.

"I have not been without this problem," she said. "When after twenty years of standing nude on a stage, inspiring dreams, I hope, in lonely men, I took the veil, it would have been very easy to assume a holy impulse—I could recite you all the ways of saying it. But I knew that I was simply tired."

"You are honest."

"I don't know. Having admitted that my impulse was less than pure, I found in myself kindnesses, understandings, that even I can find no fault with—by-products of the initial laziness—I didn't even have to worry about virtue once I took the weight off my feet."

"How about the ritual—the rising, kneeling, reciting of magic religious formulae?"

"It is no more than breathing after a little while. Easier to do than not to do."

The king got up and scratched his elbows, walked around his chair, sat down.

"It seems a big jump," he said, "from sinner to—saint."

Sister Hyacinthe laughed. "Sin is difficult to isolate in oneself," she observed. "In others it is easy to discern, but in ourselves it has a way of being based on necessity or good intentions. Please don't repeat this to Marie—"

"Pardon? Oh! I don't think it would occur to me."

"Marie is a wife—that's different."

"She is very kind to me," said the king.

Sister Hyacinthe regarded him in amazement. "I hope that was said only in courtesy," she said, "not as a truth."

"I don't know what you mean."

"There is no kindness in women," said the nun. "There is love, but that is a subjective thing. If I had ever married I might have convinced myself otherwise." She regarded him narrowly. "What is the best thing that ever happened to you, Sire?"

"Why—"

"If you can tell me, perhaps I can tell you what it is you are missing and mourning for."

"Why, I guess—I guess it was when the comet appeared in my reflector and I knew I was the first human ever to see it. I was—I was filled with wonder."

"They had no right to make you king," she said. "A king only repeats old mistakes, and if he knows this in advance—I understand now, Sire—but I can't help you. You didn't cut your wrists and now it is too late. A comet. Yes, I can see . . ."

"I like you, Sister," said the king. "Will you permit me to call on you now and then?"

"If I were sure your feeling was purely intellectual . . ."

"But Sister—"

"I should forbid it," said Sister Hyacinthe, and her laughter was reminiscent of the ladies' dressing room backstage. "You are a good man, Sire, and a good man draws women as cheese draws mice."

One of the great burdens on the king was his lack of privacy. He was followed, fawned over, protected, stared at. He had considered the use of disguises in the manner of Haroun-al-Raschid. At times he locked himself in his room simply to get away from the eyes and voices of the people who surrounded him.

At about this time he made a happy accidental discovery. The queen, finding it necessary to clean his office, sent him out until she could get it swept and dusted. He was wearing his corduroy jacket, a little frayed at the elbows, flannel trousers in need of a press, and espadrilles. He slipped some papers in a briefcase and went to the gardens to finish his work. As he sat on the coping of a fish pond, a gardener approached him.

"It is not permitted to sit here, M'sieur," said the gardener.

The king moved to a place in the shade on a great stairway. Immediately a gendarme touched his elbow.

"The visiting hours are from two to five, M'sieur. Please go to the entrance and await a guide."

Pippin gaped at him. He gathered up his papers and sauntered to the entrance. He paid his fee for the guided tour. He bought postcards and peered with the crowd into rooms guarded by velvet ropes.

All through the palace he saw servants and nobility and ministers of state and not one of them looked at the man in the corduroy jacket and espadrilles. Even the queen bustled by and did not notice him as the tour stared after her.

In delight he followed the tourists back to the entrance and boarded the chartered bus for Paris. His heart was light. To test himself thoroughly he strolled up the Champs Elysées and no one saw him.

He took a table at the Select and ordered a Pernod and water and he watched the passing throng. He listened to tourist talk, and his freedom grew on him like wings.

He indulged himself in a mildly anti-monarchist argument with a correspondent from *Life* magazine, who retorted, "I suppose the king hasn't yet been able to clean out all the Communists."

Pippin sneered, borrowed a cigarette, and strolled across the Champs Elysées, past Fouquet's, and into the Avenue George V, past the Hotel Prince de Galles, and to the entrance of the Hotel George V itself. As he entered the lobby, he was stopped by an official.

"You wish something?"

"I wish to see Mr. Tod Johnson."

"You are delivering something? Leave it at the—"

"I have his briefcase," said Pippin. "He has asked me to hand it to him personally."

"The hall porter—" began the official, his eyes fastened on the espadrilles.

"Please call Mr. Tod Johnson's suite, M'sieur. Tell him that Mr. King has brought his briefcase from Uncle Charlie's Gallery."

Tod welcomed Pippin at the door to his apartment, tipped the suspicious guide, and clapped the king on the back.

"Well, I'll be damned," he said.

"Isn't it wonderful? I had a hard time getting in," said the king.

Tod said, "I have a friend who claims that, if you want to hide, get a job as a waiter in a good restaurant. No one ever looks at a waiter. Sit down, sir. Can I get you a drink?"

"A—how do you call it?—mar—mart—?"

"Martini?"

"Exactly, a martini," said the king happily. "Do you know, a tourist nearly had me arrested for lèse majesté."

"Won't they be looking for you, sir?"

"I hope so," said the king. "But they won't look here. You said yourself that the French do not come here. . . . Now that, my friend, is a better one than my uncle makes."

"He can't bring himself to use enough ice," said Tod.

"One of my own guards ejected me from my own garden," said the king happily.

"I guess people see what they expect to see. They don't expect a bareheaded king with a bald spot. Did you think of it yourself, sir?"

"Oh, no! It was an accident. You see, Marie wanted to clean my little office. And then a gardener wouldn't let me sit down on a coping."

"You aren't insulted?"

"How do you mean, insulted? I've never been happier."

"Well, I know some great stars of Hollywood who disguise themselves with dark glasses and pulled-down hats. They're pretty upset if no one recognizes them. Then there's the owner of three of our biggest magazines. He has a real hatred for publicity but he just happens to get photographed all the time. Take my father, now—"

Pippin broke in. "I wanted to talk to you about your father."

"Had a long letter from him this morning. He doesn't approve of me going around with Bugsy, with the princess."

"He doesn't?"

"No. He's a snob. You see, he's a self-made man, and there's no snob like a self-made man. They say he only looks up to his maker. The second generation can relax a little—even be democratic.

"My father's letter is funny. He's interested in what is going on here. He says for me to tell you that you've got a real chance here, if you play your cards right. But he doesn't believe you will."

"Do you think he would come here to advise me?"

"Oh, no!" said Tod. "He's a snob. He might come over later and criticize. There's a dividend here." And Tod filled the king's glass.

"I came to see you because I want to ask you some questions. It is true that at first your father actually raised chickens?"

"Sure he did, and he hates chickens."

"Is it not also true that many of the heads of your greatest corporations worked up from the bottom? I seem to remember . . ."

"Sure. Knudsen was an iron puddler; Ben Fairless worked on an open hearth, I think. I could name you lots—Charlie Wilson— oh, lots!"

"Then they know their business on all levels—"

"True," said Tod. "But don't think that makes them democratic. It's just the opposite."

"I've never understood America," said the king.

"Neither do we, sir. You might say we have two governments, kind of overlapping. First we have the elected government. It's Democratic or Republican, doesn't make much difference, and then there's corporation government."

"They get along together, these governments?"

"Sometimes," said Tod. "I don't understand it myself. You see, the elected government pretends to be democratic, and actually it is autocratic. The corporation governments pretend to be autocratic and they're all the time accusing the others of socialism. They hate socialism."

"So I have heard," said Pippin.

"Well, here's the funny thing, sir. You take a big corporation in America, say like General Motors or Du Pont or U.S. Steel. The thing they're most afraid of is socialism, and at the same time they themselves are socialist states."

The king sat bolt upright. "Please?" he said.

"Well, just look at it, sir. They've got medical care for employees and their families and accident insurance and retirement pensions, paid vacations—even vacation places—and they're beginning to get guaranteed pay over the year. The employees have representation in pretty nearly everything, even the color they paint the factories. As a matter of fact, they've got socialism that makes the USSR look silly. Our corporations make the U.S. Government seem like an absolute monarchy. Why, if the U.S. government tried to do one-tenth of what General Motors does, General Motors would go into armed revolt. It's what you might call a paradox, sir."

Pippin shook his head. He got up and went to the window and looked down on the tree-shaded Avenue George V. "Can you explain why they do these things?" he asked.

Tod Johnson poured gin by eye into the tall mixer, dashed a few drops of vermouth in, and stirred ice cubes round and round in the mixture.

"That is the oddest thing of all and the most reasonable," he said. "Do you like a squeeze of lemon peel, sir?"

"Yes, please. But why?"

"They don't do it out of kindness, sir. It's just that some of them have found out they can produce and sell more goods that way. They used to fight the employees. That's expensive. And sick workers are expensive. Do you think my father likes to feed his chickens vitamins and cod-liver oil and minerals and keep them warm and dry and happy? Hell, no! They lay more eggs that way. Oh, it wasn't quick and it's far from finished, but isn't it strange, sir, that out of the most autocratic system in the world the only really workable socialism seems to be growing? If my father heard me say that he'd string me up by the thumbs. He thinks *he* makes the decisions."

"And who does, Tod?"

"Circumstances and pressures," said Tod. "If he hadn't gone along with the pressures he wouldn't be in business." He drained the new martini gently into the glasses. "I'm going to send for a sandwich, sir. These things are murder if you don't eat."

The king sipped at his drink. "These changes didn't come easily?"

"Hell, no. It took about a hundred years and a lot of fighting, and some of it is still going on." Tod laughed gently. "You know, sir, I think my old man's itching to get his fingers on this operation. He wrote me nine pages in his letter, mostly questions to ask you. When my old man asks a question, he's telling you."

The king said dreamily, "Perhaps I had better wait for the sandwich before I hear the questions. How do you get along with—what do you call her, Bugsy?"

"It's kind of off and on, sir. I'm fond of her, but every once in a while when she goes royal on me I want to kick her in the pants."

"She matured early," said Pippin. "By the time she was eighteen she had lived several lives."

"That's just it. She didn't have a decent adolescence when she was fourteen and fifteen, and now it's snapping back at her. She jumps from little kid to Mrs. Astor, back and forth."

Pippin said a little thickly, "I am basically a scientist, and a scientist is or should be an observer. Now, young sir, the artistic, the creative side of a scientist indulges in hypothesis.

Watching Clotilde and her friends, I have formulated a maturity hypothesis." His speech had the slow precision of mild intoxication. "Those drinks are very strong," he said.

"It's not their strength, it's their inherent meanness," said Tod. "Look, King, you've got me talking that way too. What's your maturity business?"

Pippin's eyes had closed, but they opened a slit and he shook his head as though his ears were full of water. "The human fetus is born upside down," he said solemnly. "But it is not true that a child becomes upright after birth. Observe the feet of children and young people when they are at rest. The feet are nearly always higher than the head. No matter how hard he may try, the growing boy, and particularly girl, cannot keep the feet down. The fetal position is very strong. It takes eighteen to twenty years for the feet finally to accept the ground as their normal home. It is my hypothesis that you can judge maturity exactly by the relationship of the feet to the ground."

Tod laughed. "I have a sister—" he began.

The king suddenly arose. "Please—" he said, "please direct me to the—"

Tod leaped up and took his arm. "This way, sir," he said. "Here—let me help you. Mind the little step here."

The dawn was breaking when the king awakened in one of Tod's twin beds. He looked in wonder about the room. "Où suis-je?" he asked plaintively.

"You're all right, King," said Tod from the other bed. "How do you feel?"

"Feel?" said the king. "Why—all—I feel all right."

"I loaded you with aspirin and B_1 tablets," said Tod. "Sometimes that will head off a hangover."

The king sat up. "My God!—Marie! She'll have the police out."

"Take it easy," said Tod. "I telephoned Bugsy."

"What did you tell her?"

"I told her you were drunk," said Tod.

"But Marie?"

"Don't worry, sir. The princess has informed Her Majesty that you are in a top-secret conference with Your Majesty's ministers—a matter of international importance."

"You're a good boy," said the king. "I ought to make you a minister."

"I've got enough trouble," said Tod. "Did you ever have a Bloody Mary?"

"What is that?"

"Had to change the name in France. You had no Queen Mary in France, so the name seemed a little sacrilegious. Here it is called Marie Blessée."

"Wounded Mary," said the king. "What is it?"

"Leave it in my hands, sir. It is elixir, it is pretty close to a transfusion." He reached for the telephone. "Louis? Tod Johnson ici. Quatre Maries Blessées, s'il vous plaît. Vite. Oui—quatre. Très bien. Merci bien."

"You speak abominable French," said the king.

"I know," said Tod. "I won't be surprised if Louis sends four wounded girls." And then he said irritably. "You might have a little trouble with language in New York, King."

"But I speak English."

"They don't," said Tod, and he went to the door to receive the tray of Bloody Marys.

By nine o'clock the king had recovered, and a little more.

"I should go back," he said.

"Make the most of it, sir. You may never get out again."

"You must beware of my Uncle Charles," said Pippin. "There are times when I feel he is not quite—"

"He certainly isn't—but do you know, sir, he hasn't sold me a single picture. He is charmed with my resistance. He admires me. Do you feel well enough now to hear some of my father's questions?"

The king sighed. "I suppose so. I wish I could forget the throne for a little while. I would rather be a corporation. Are all of your pajamas silk, my friend?"

"No, the ones you have on are my social pajamas. I sleep in a T-shirt. It doesn't bind.

"My father says you've got to break it down. He always says you've got to break everything down. What have you got to sell and who is going to buy it and have they got the money?"

"Sell?"

"Sure—now we sell eggs and pullets and supplies."

"What has a government to sell? It is a government."

"Sure, I know, but it has to sell something or you wouldn't need a government."

The king frowned. "I hadn't thought of it that way. Well, perhaps peace, order—perhaps progress, happiness."

"That's quite a business," said Tod. "Now my father wants to know have you the capital and organization to do it?"

"I have the throne."

Tod said, "Seems to me the throne has some assets but it has some liabilities too. Take that bunch of freeloaders out at your place. You ought to get rid of them. They'll eat up the profit."

"But they are the nobility, the foundation of the throne."

"More like termites in the foundation. Maybe if you had a sinking fund you could pension them off. One thing is sure, you can't put them to work."

"Heavens, no!"

"How did they get to be nobles in the first place?"

"By service to the throne," said the king. "Spiritual, military, financial."

"There—you see? Those old boys weren't stupid. Now spiritual is taken care of, military is out of your hands, but financial— you could use."

"Most of the nobility through misfortune—"

"Are broke," said Tod. "So let's put them out to pasture and get in a new crop."

"I don't understand."

"Look, King, I could sell titles in Texas and Beverly Hills for anything I want to ask. Why, I know people who would give the bottom dollar of a big stack for a patent of nobility."

"That isn't right."

"What do you mean, right? That's how these boys got it. The British still do it. You don't have to own a distillery to sit in the House of Lords, but it helps."

"My friend, you are speaking of tradition."

Tod said, "The Dukedom of Dallas?—why, ten billionaires would be after it. I could do it by sealed bid. Only trouble is the Earl of Fort Worth might declare war on the Duke of Dallas. Say, this is wonderful! I can see those dames snooting each other. All they've got to throw at each other now is oil wells and air conditioning."

"You make jokes, my friend."

"Don't you believe it! Drink up, King, and I'll order another round. These things don't trick you like martinis."

"Don't—shouldn't we have some breakfast?"

"Breakfast is right in them—good healthy tomato juice, and then there's liver in Worcestershire."

"Well, in that case—" said the king.

"How about it? We can put out the word privately like a stock issue—dignified."

"I believe," said the king, "that you have laws forbidding your citizens to hold titles."

"Forget it," said Tod. "If those oil and cattle boys can rig the tax laws and the utilities laws, they aren't going to have any trouble with a little old law against titles. We could guarantee a knighthood for every congressman who voted in favor—but the big titles, that's where the money is."

The king said, "I have met some Texans. They seemed very democratic. In fact, they usually announce themselves as 'little old country boys.'"

"Yes, King, and those little old country boys usually have half a million acres, three airplanes, a yacht, and a house in Cannes. But we don't have to limit it to Texas. Think of Los Angeles, and when we've worked that over there's Brazil, Argentina—the field is unlimited."

"The whole thing smacks of my uncle," said the king.

"Well, I did discuss it with him. There's pots in it, King. I can arrange the whole thing."

The king was silent so long that Tod looked at him in alarm. "You feel bad again, sir?"

Pippin was staring straight ahead and, although his eyes crossed slightly, his chin was firm and his bearing regal.

"You have forgotten, my friend, that the purpose of a king is the well-being of his people—all of his people."

"I know," said Tod. "But it's like my father says. You've got to have capital and organization. The people who put you in didn't do it for nothing. Sooner or later you're going to have to fight them or join them."

"How about simple honesty—simple logic?"

"That has never worked," said Tod. "I hate to remind you of your own history. Louis the Fourteenth was a spendthrift. He busted the nation. He was at war all the time. He drained the treasury and wiped out a generation of young men. But he was the Sun King and he was adored, while France was flat on its pants.

"Then along came Louis the Sixteenth and he was simple and honest. He brought in efficiency experts. He called assemblies, he tried to listen, to understand. He tried everything and—" Tod drew his hand across his throat.

Pippin's head sank on his chest. He said sadly, "Why did they have to make me king?"

"I'm sorry," said Tod. "I guess I haven't helped much. But you get a thing like a throne in your hands and pretty soon you want to use it."

"I want peace—and my telescope."

"You'll want to use it," said Tod. "Everyone does. Look, I've been lousy to you. Let's you and me go out on the town and see how the other half lives."

"I must go back."

"But you may never break loose again. Besides, you owe it to your people to associate with them."

"Well, if you put it that way."

"I'll lend you some clothes," said Tod. "Nobody will ever recognize you."

"Do you want to call Clotilde?"

"No," said Tod. "Let you and me stag it."

———

At three-thirty in the morning, the Life Guard, Lieutenant Emile de Samothrace, on duty at the gate of Versailles, was alerted by a disturbance in front of the palace. In the half-darkness he was able to discern two men who clung solicitously together while they marched to the gate, singing:

> *"Allons, enfants de la Patrie*
> *All the livelong day.*
> *Le jour de gloire est arrivé*
> *And the monkey wrapped his tail*
> *around the flagpole.*
> *Baa! Baa! Baa!"*

Lieutenant de Samothrace intercepted the two while he shouted for the guard, whereupon they charged him with umbrellas, shrieking, "To the Bastille!"

The lieutenant's report read: "One of these men claimed to be Crown Prince of Petaluma while the other continued to mutter 'Baa! Baa! Baa!' I turned them over to the commandant of the palace for questioning."

The next evening, coming on duty, the lieutenant found that his report had been removed from the book and in its place was the notation: "Three hours and thirty minutes and all is well." And it was initialed by the commandant.

Lieutenant de Samothrace found that the words of the song kept running through his head. "Baa! Baa! Baa!"

And meanwhile France enjoyed such peace and prosperity and profit that the newspapers began to refer to the time as the Platinum Age. The New York *Daily News* called Pippin "The Atomic King." The *Reader's Digest* reprinted three articles it had commissioned: one in the *Saturday Evening Post*, called "Royalty Re-examined"; one in the *Ladies' Home Journal*, "The Glorious Present," and one in the *American Legion Monthly*, "A King against Communism."

Citroën announced a new model.

Christian Dior introduced the R line with the highest waistline and the most bursting bodice since Montesquieu.

The Italian Couture out of jealousy maintained that the R line made breasts look like goiters. Gina Lollobrigida, always

loyal to Italy, said, on arriving at Idlewild en route to Hollywood, that she refused to look out between herself. But criticism of France was largely grounded in envy of the Platinum
Age.

England smoldered and waited.

The Soviet Purchasing Agency ordered four tank cars of
French perfume.

In America the excitement rose to fever pitch. Bonwit Teller
named one whole floor L'Etage Royal.

A benevolent autumn slipped warmly over France, moved
up-Seine and then up-Loire, spread over the Dordogne, climbed
the Jura, and lapped against the Alps. A great wheat crop
had been harvested, and the grapes were warm and fat and
happy. Even the truffles were benevolent—black and full, almost leaping out of the limestone earth. In the north the cows
staggered cream-heavy in the pasturage, while the apple crop
for once was ready and sufficient for the champagne the English love.

At no time in history had the tourists been so open-handed
and humble nor their French hosts so happily sullen.

International relations reached fraternal heights. The most
conservative peasants bought new corduroy pants. The red
rivers of Bordeaux flowed from the wine presses. The sheep
gave milk of a milkness for the cheese.

Vacations being over, parties and sub-parties met in Paris to
complete their contributions to the Code Pippin to be adopted
in November.

The Christian Atheists achieved a clause imposing an amusement tax on church services. The Christian Christians were
ready with a law for compulsory attendance of mass.

Right and Left Centrists walked arm in arm.

Communists and Socialists took to raising their hats to one
another.

M. Deuxcloches, Cultural Custodian, but actual leader of
the Communist party of France, put into words what every
party was thinking. Speaking in secret caucus, he outlined a series of traps and deadfalls so artfully conceived that no possible
move by the king could avoid being disastrous.

France was on a peak of good fortune. Everyone admitted it. Tourists were sleeping in the flowerbeds of the better hotels.

This being so, how does one explain the little cloud that peered over the horizon in mid-September, blackened and spread during the first weeks of October, towered like a thunderhead as November approached?

It is common to explain historic events after the fact in terms of the preoccupation of the historian. Thus the economist finds his pattern in economics, the politician in politics, the medical man in pollens or parasites. Very few if any historians have looked for causes simply in how people feel about things. Is it not true that in the United States the eras of greatest peace and prosperity have been also the periods of greatest uneasiness and discontent? Is it not also true that in these weeks of France's fruition there began to develop and grow among all classes a restlessness, a nervousness, a rustle of fear?

If this should seem unreasonable, even unbelievable, consider to yourself how on a lovely sunny day a man will say to his neighbor, "Probably rain tomorrow." How in a cold, damp winter the general opinion is that it will be a hot, dry summer. Who has not heard a farmer, looking at his abundant crop, complain, "There won't be any market"?

I do not think the historian need look any further in this. It is the tendency of human beings to distrust good fortune. In evil times we are too busy protecting ourselves. We are equipped for this. The one thing our species is helpless against is good fortune. It first puzzles, then frightens, then angers, and finally destroys us. Our basic conviction was put into words by a great and illiterate third baseman.

"Everything in life," he said, "is seven to five against."

The peasant, counting his profits, found time to wonder how much he had lost to the wholesaler. The retail merchant could be heard to curse under his breath when the wholesaler turned his back.

This climate of suspicion on an individual level did not remain there. For example, the Foreign Policy Committee of the United States Senate, hearing of the Russian purchase of four tank cars of French perfume, requested samples from the Secret

Service and put them in the hands of qualified scientists to find what offensive qualities—explosive, poisonous, or hypnotic—might lurk in "Quatre-Vingt Fleurs" or the newest product, "L'Eau d'Eau."

On the other hand, Russian operatives secretly inspected a shipment of plastic helicopters designed for the toy shops of Paris.

A troop of French Boy Scouts, drilling with quarter-staffs, was photographed by the silent services of four nations and the pictures sent home for evaluation.

Worst badgered of all were the speleologists, who found that they could not be alone and unobserved even in the deepest caves.

Suspicion of France was on the rise throughout the world. And in France there were gusts of nervousness. Luxembourg's addition of eight soldiers to its standing army caused a hurried meeting in the Quai d'Orsay.

In the provinces, people glanced nervously in the direction of Paris. In Paris it was whispered that the provinces were growing increasingly restless.

Armed robbery increased. Juvenile delinquency skyrocketed.

When on September 17 the police discovered in a cellar on the Ile Saint-Louis a cache of buried Communist arms, a ripple of terror spread through France. The police perhaps were not sufficiently explicit. They did not make public that the arms had been hidden by the Commune of 1871, that the cap-and-ball rifles and ancient bayonets were not only obsolete but heavily rusted.

And while this cloud was rising and darkening—what of the king?

It is generally agreed that within a short time of his coronation the king began to change. Such a thing was to be expected, or at least to be anticipated.

Let us draw a parallel. Consider a strain of bird dogs, say pointers, developed, selected, and trained for a thousand generations for the trait of hunting. Then imagine a morganatic marriage and a resulting intermixture of blood until finally we have a puppy of this mingling in a pet-shop window. He is taken to live in a city apartment, walked twice a day on leash, sniffing his way from automobile tire to trash basket to fire hydrant. His nose is accustomed to perfume, gasoline, and mothballs. His toenails are clipped; his skin scented with pine soap; his food taken from a tin can.

This dog, growing up, is trained perhaps to carry the morning paper from the apartment door, to sit, to lie down, to shake hands, to beg, to bring his master's slippers. He is disciplined to stay clear of the hors-d'oeuvre tray, to control his bladder. The only birds he has ever known are fat waddling pigeons, or frantic sparrows in the street; the only love a sneer from a passing Pekingese.

Let us then suppose that in his prime of life this dog—the descendant of greatness—is taken on a picnic in the country, to a pleasant place beside a little stream. In the war against sand and ants and the winds which whip up the corners of the tablecloth, our dog is forgotten for a moment.

He smells the lusciousness of running water and strolls to the streamside and drinks deeply of a fluid uninfused with germicides. An ancient feeling fills his breast. He moves along a little path, sniffing at leaves and brown tree trunks and at grass. He pauses at a track where a rabbit has crossed. The fresh wind teases his skin.

Suddenly an emotion falls upon him: an ecstasy, a fullness, like a memory. To his nose comes a scent unknown but remembered. He shivers and makes a little whining sound, then moves uncertainly toward the magic.

Then hypnosis falls upon him. His shoulders hunch a little. His thin tail straightens. One foot creeps after its fellow. His neck stretches forward until nose and head and spine and tail become one line. His right front paw rises. He freezes. He does not breathe. His body is like a compass needle, or like a gun pointing at a covey of quail hidden in the underbrush.

In February 19— a gentle, inquisitive man lived in a small house in Avenue de Marigny, together with his daughter and his pleasant wife, his balcony and his telescope, his rubbers and umbrella, and his briefcase always. He had dentists, and insurance, and a little stock in the Crédit Lyonnais. A vineyard in Auxerre . . .

Then without warning this little man was made king. Who of us who do not have the blood can know what happened at Reims when the royal crown descended? Did Paris look the same to the king as it had to the amateur astronomer? How did the word "France" sound in the ears of the king?—and the word "People" in the ears of the king?

It would be strange if ancient mechanisms failed to operate. Perhaps the king did not know what was happening. Perhaps he, like the pointer, responded to forgotten stimuli. It seems undeniable that the kingdom created a king.

Once he became the king he was alone, set apart and alone, and this is a part of being a king. Monarchy created a king.

Uncle Charlie had been to Versailles once in his life when as a child in black smock and white collar he marched in a ragged line of smocked schoolchildren through halls and bedchambers, ballrooms and cellars of that national monument, on order of the Minister of Public Instruction.

At that time Charles conceived a hatred and horror for the royal palace from which he never recovered. He remembered the cracked and painted paneling, the squeaking parquetry, the velvet ropes, the drafty halls, as a kind of nightmare.

It was, therefore, a surprise to the king when Uncle Charlie called on him in the royal apartments, and even a greater surprise that he was accompanied by Tod Johnson.

Charles gazed about the painted room. The floors screamed with shrunken pain when he moved. A blanket was tacked over the windows to keep the chill autumn winds out, and a log fire burned in the great fireplace. The gilt clocks sat on their marble tables and the stiff chairs stood against the wall as Charles remembered them.

Uncle Charlie said, "I must speak to you, my child."

Tod broke in. "I read in the Paris *Herald Tribune* that you had a mistress, sir. Art Buchwald said it."

The king raised his eyebrows.

Uncle Charlie said quickly, "I am teaching Tod my business. He's opening a branch in Beverly Hills."

"You can sell them anything as long as the price is high," said Tod. "Where do you keep your mistress, sir?"

"I have made some changes," the king said, "but in the matter of a mistress I had to compromise. The feeling was too strong. She is a nice little woman, I am told. Does her job well."

"You were told, sir? Haven't you seen her?"

"No," said the king, "I haven't. The queen insists that I ask her for an aperitif one day soon. Everyone says she is very nice; dresses well—neat, pleasant. It's just a form, but in this business forms are very important, particularly if one has plans."

"Aha," said Uncle Charlie. "Plans. That's just what I was afraid of. That's why I came."

"What do you mean?" the king asked mildly.

"Listen, my child. Do you think your secret is a secret? All Paris, all France knows."

"Knows what?"

"My dear nephew, did you think a mechanic's jumper and a false mustache was a disguise? Do you think, when you applied for a job at Citroën and stood all day at the gates talking to the workmen, that you were actually incognito? And when you went through the old buildings on the Left Bank, pretending to be an inspector, tapping on walls, looking down drains—did you imagine that anyone thought you were an inspector?"

"I am amazed," said the king. "I had the cap, the badge."

"And it's not only that," cried Uncle Charlie. "You've been out in the vineyards, pretending to be a vine-dresser. You have driven the concessionaires at Les Halles insane with your questioning." He mimicked, "'What do you pay for carrots? What do you sell them for? What does the wholesaler pay the farmer for them?' And the working man: 'What rent do you pay? What are your wages? How much do you pay to the union?

What benefits do you get? What is your average cost for food and rent for the week?' I think there you pretended to be a reporter from *L'Humanité.*"

"I had a press card," said the king.

"Pippin," demanded Uncle Charlie, "what are you up to? I warn you! People are growing nervous."

The king tried to pace the floor until the squealing of the inlaid wood stopped him. He removed his pince-nez and straddled it on the forefinger of his left hand.

"I was trying to learn. There are so many things to be done. Did you know, Uncle Charlie, that twenty per cent of the rented buildings of Paris are a danger to health as well as a threat to safety? Only last week a family in Montmartre was nearly smothered with falling plaster. Do you know that the wholesaler takes thirty per cent of the selling price of those same carrots and the retailer takes forty per cent? And do you know what that leaves for the farmer who raises a bunch of carrots?"

"Stop!" cried Uncle Charlie. "Stop right there! You are playing with fire. Do you want barricades in the streets again? Do you wish Paris in flames? What makes you think you can reduce the numbers of the captains of police?"

"Nine out of ten of them do nothing," said the king.

"Oh, my child," said Uncle Charlie. "My poor bewildered child. You are not going to fall into the old trap, are you? Study the British. When the present Duke of Windsor was king he went down into a coal mine just once and the resulting shock not only caused questions in Parliament but nearly lost the prime minister a vote of confidence. Pippin, my dear, dear child, I order you to desist!"

The king sat down in a little chair and it became a throne.

"I did not ask to be king," he said, "but I am king and I find this dear, rich, productive France torn by selfish factions, fleeced by greedy promoters, deceived by parties. I find that there are six hundred ways of avoiding taxes if you are rich enough—sixty-five methods of raising rent in controlled rental areas. The riches of France, which should have some kind of distribution, are gobbled up. Everyone robs everyone, until a level is reached where there is nothing left to steal. No new houses are built and the old ones are falling to pieces. And on this favored land the maggots are feeding."

"Pippin, stop it!"

"I am a king, Uncle Charlie. Please do not forget that. I know now why confusion in government is not only tolerated but encouraged. I have learned. A confused people can make no clear demands.

"Do you know what a French workman or peasant says when he refers to the government? He calls it 'them.' *They* are doing this. *They, they, they.* Something set apart, nameless, unidentifiable, and so unattackable. Anger dwindles down to grumbling. How can you force redress from something which does not exist?

"And consider the intellectuals, the dried-up minds. The writers in the past burned the name 'France' on the world. Do you know what they are doing now? They're sitting in huddled misery, building a philosophy of despair, while the painters, with few exceptions, paint apathy and jealous anarchy."

Uncle Charlie sat on the edge of one of the brocaded chairs and he rested his head in his cupped hands and he swayed from side to side like a mourner at a funeral.

Tod Johnson stood at the fireplace, warming his back. He asked quietly, "Have you got the capital and organization to change it?"

"He's got nothing," Uncle Charlie moaned. "Not one person. Not one sou."

"I have the Crown," said Pippin.

"They'll have you in the tumbril. Don't think the guillotine is beyond recall. You'll fail before you start. They'll destroy you."

"You use the word yourself," said Pippin. "*They, they,* the nameless *they.* It seems to me that even though the king may know he will fail, the king must try."

"Not so, my child. Not so. There have been many kings who simply sat back and—"

"I don't believe it," said the king. "I believe they tried, whatever was said of them. They must have tried; every one of them must have tried."

"How about a war?" Charlie suggested.

The king chuckled. "I know you have my welfare at heart, dear Uncle."

"Come on, Tod," said Charles Martel. "Let's get the hell out of here."

"I want to talk to Tod," said Pippin. "Good night, dear Uncle. You can go down that staircase in the corner and avoid the aristocrats. Creep out through the garden. Give the Royal Guard a cigarette!"

After Charles had gone, Pippin raised a corner of the blanket and peered out. The chill night was full of frog sounds and the carp were burping and spluttering in the ponds. He saw his unfortunate uncle moving along the path, his arm clutched by an elderly nobleman who spoke earnestly and loudly in Gothic type into Charles's ear.

The king sighed and dropped the blanket and turned back to Tod. "Such a pessimist," said Pippin. "He never married, you know. He always said that by the time he knew the woman well enough to marry her, he knew better."

"He's an operator," said Tod. "But you know he didn't really want to enlarge his business. I had to guarantee it wouldn't be any work or trouble to him."

The king pressed the edge of the blanket against the chill from the window. "The frames are shrunk," he said. "Marie hates to have me put the blanket up—but I get cold."

"How about plastic wood?" said Tod. "It's a kind of putty."

Pippin observed, "Modern repairs for an old structure. Now that's one of the reasons I asked you to wait. Perhaps my memory is a little cloudy about our last meeting."

"But sir—"

"It was very pleasant and it did help me. I believe you lectured me about American corporations—"

"I don't know much about them, sir, but, you see, our family *is* a corporation and so naturally—"

"I understand. Now your government is a democracy—a system of checks and balances. Is that not right?"

"Right, sir," said Tod.

"And within that structure you have great corporations

which themselves have somewhat the nature of governments. Is that not also right?"

"You're ahead of me, sir, but I guess that's right. You've been burning brain juice."

"Thank you. I guess I have. Is it not so that there is in a corporation a, shall we say, flexibility, one does not find in your government? I mean, could not a change of policy be carried out quickly and effectively in a corporation, let us say by an order from the chairman of the board, without consulting all of the stockholders, an order which is presumed to be for the good and profit of the shareholders?"

Tod regarded the sovereign with speculative eyes. "I see what you're getting at, sir."

"What would be the procedure?"

"You think you might get further as chairman of the board than as king?"

"I am asking, perhaps, a leading question."

"Well, let me think, sir. If it was a big change the chairman would put the question up to the board members, and if they agreed the order would go out. If they split, they'd have to call on the stockholders."

"I guess that's out of the question, then," said the king. "I can't get even two of our people to agree."

"You see, sir," said Tod, "each member of the board represents a certain amount of stock. If there's a rhubarb, the members vote proxies from the stockholders. The one with the most proxies gets control. Then the unions must be consulted if they have a beef."

"Oh, dear! Even for a program obviously good and desirable?"

"Yes, sir. You might say particularly then."

The king sighed. "Apparently a corporation isn't much different from a government."

"Well, it's a little different. It depends on how the stock is held. All the stock in our corporation is held by our family. Remember when we talked about selling titles in America?"

"Through a haze I remember it."

"There's a fortune in it," cried Tod. "Why, sir, it might solve this proxy business. Why don't you just put it in my hands? I can get a hundred thousand dollars for a little old knighthood. I'll bet I can sell a dukedom for anything I want to ask."

The king held up his hand.

"Now wait," said Tod, "listen to this. I can put it in the patent that you keep the proxy. Why, it's better than a stock division. I can get Neiman-Marcus in back of it. It will be bigger than Miss Rheingold and the Academy Awards and the Aquacade put together."

The king said, "Don't you call that watering the stock?"

"Oh, no!" cried Tod. "It's better than that. More like a reissue—kind of refinancing. Maybe Billy Rose would produce it. He's looking around for something big."

The king had sunk his head deep between his shoulders. He shivered. And then he chuckled. "I, Pippin the Fourth, King of France, find that I can only talk to a rich young tourist and an old nun who used to be a chorus girl."

Tod asked, "Is it true what Uncle Charlie said, sir? Have you been going around in disguises?"

"It was a mistake," said the king. "When I visited you no one saw me. The caps and mustaches and badges were a mistake."

"Why did you do it, sir?"

"I thought it might be a good idea to know something about France. Have you noticed a chill in the air?"

"Well, in a way. There's a lot of talk."

"I know," said the king. "I've heard it."

"There's one thing that makes me feel bad," said Tod. "My father—"

"He is ill?"

"You might call it that. He's got duke fever—of all the people in the world."

"Maybe there's a little of it in all of us, Tod."

"But you don't understand—my father—"

"Perhaps I do—a little," said the king.

———

As the autumnal days grew shorter, more and more private au-
diences were asked or even demanded of the king. Then he
would sit behind his audience desk in a room that had been
built and embellished for another king, while two or three representatives of faction or interest spoke to him privately. Each
deputation was confident that the king was their partisan. They
never came alone. The thought drifted through Pippin's mind
that they did not trust one another. Every one of the representatives had the good of France at heart, but it was also true
that the ultimate good of France rested on the primary good of
faction—or even individual.

In this manner the king learned what was in store for France,
what plans were being made. He sat silently and listened while
Socialists proved that Communists must be outlawed, while
Centrists showed beyond doubt that only if the financial back-
bone of France were bolstered and defended could prosperity
trickle down to the lower orders.

Religionists and anti-Religionists each made their irrefutable
points.

The king listened silently. And he emerged depressed.

Pippin's mind often sought shelter in the memory of his little
balcony in the Avenue de Marigny. He could see and feel the
dark and silent sky and the slow-flailing nebulae.

Outwardly he was calm and friendly. Now and then he nodded
his head, which the audience took to mean the king's agreement and which was actually only the king's growing knowledge of government and of kingship.

He accepted loneliness, but he could not control a scurrying
search for either solution or escape, and he did not find them
anywhere.

Where the partisans left off the ambassadors continued. Sitting in his painted room, Pippin politely heard the neat and
statesmanlike ambitions of other nations to use France, each
for its own purpose—and again he nodded and gray depression
fogged his soul.

On November 15 the various parties to be represented in the
Constitutional Convention petitioned the crown to set the date

for convening ahead to December 5. The king graciously agreed, and it was so ordered.

In the evenings Pippin took to making notes in the small lined copybooks which in other days he had used to log the heavens.

Madame Marie was worried about him. "He is so listless— so detached," she told Sister Hyacinthe. "It's not like his old detachment. He asked me yesterday if I liked being queen— *liked!*"

"What did you say?" the nun asked.

"I told what is true, that I had never thought of it one way or another. I just do what each day demands."

"Well, did you like *not* being queen?"

"It was perhaps easier," said the queen, "but not much different. A clean, well-run house is the same everywhere, and husbands are husbands—kings or astronomers. But I think M'sieur is sad."

Chill mornings came, with heartening sunshine in the midday. The leaves fell from chestnuts and plane trees, and the street-sweepers' brooms were busy.

The king went back to his original disguise, which was himself. Dressed in his corduroy jacket and espadrilles, he took to riding a motor scooter about the country. After two falls he added a crash helmet to his costume.

One day he scooted to the little town of Gambais, famous for its perfect if partly ruined Château de Neuville. Pippin ate his lunch beside the overgrown moat of the château. He watched an elderly man feeling about in the reedy water of the moat with a long-tined rake.

The old man made contact with a hard and heavy object, and dragged it up the bank. It was a mossy bust of Pan, horned and garlanded. Only when the ancient struggled to lift Pan to a granite pedestal on the moat's edge did the king get up and move to help him. The two of them heaved the heavy statue up on its base, and then they stood back and regarded it, wiping their green and slippery fingers on their trousers.

"I like it facing a little more east," the old man said. The two of them edged it around. Pippin with his handkerchief wiped the crusted Panic face until the feral lips and the sly, lecherous eyes were visible.

"How did he get in the moat?" the king asked.

"Oh, someone pushed him in. They always do, sometimes two or three times a year."

"But why?"

The old man raised his shoulders and spread his hands. "Who knows?" he said. "There's people that push things in the moat. Pretty hard work too. There's just people that push things in the moat. See those other stands along there? There's a marble vase and a baby with a shell and a Leda in the water down there."

"I wonder why they do it—angry, do you think?"

"Who knows? It's what they do—creep in at night."

"And you always pull them out?"

"I'm late this year. I've had too much to do, and rheumatism."

"Why don't you anchor the statues to the bases?"

"Why, don't you see," the old man explained patiently, "then they'd push the base in too. I don't know if I could manage to get them out then."

The king asked gently, "Are you the owner here?"

"No, I'm not. I live hereabouts."

"Then why do you pull them out?"

The old man looked puzzled—searched for an answer. "Why—I don't know. I guess there's people that pull things out—that's what they do. I guess I'm one of that kind."

The king stared at the green, slimy Pan.

The old man said helplessly, "I guess there's people that do different things, and," he added as though he had just discovered it, "I guess that's how things get done."

"Good or bad?" the king asked.

"I don't understand," said the old man helplessly. "There's just people—just what people do."

———

The king often called on Sister Hyacinthe, sometimes to speak quietly of the day's happenings and at other times to sit silently. And she, who had had more—if different—experience than Marie, knew when to chatter and when to join him in a healing quietness.

Once she told him, "I wonder what the Superior would think if she knew that, with one exception, I am fulfilling the functions of the king's mistress. You really should see your mistress, Sire. She feels left out. She had to struggle with her soul to become your mistress, and now she finds the struggle in vain. You haven't even spoken to her, let alone seduced her."

"Later," said the king. "Perhaps later I'll ask her to tea—what is her name again?"

After returning from Gambais, the king went without announcement to call on Sister Hyacinthe, and he found her in the midst of her massage. All he could see of her were two pink feet and ankles protruding through the holes in the screen.

"He's almost finished, Sire," her voice said from behind the partition.

The master bowed and went back to his work, making little mewing sounds of affection and respect over the pink toes, giving pats and squeezes of encouragement to her flattened arches.

"I see an improvement," he said professionally. And to the king, "Regard, Sire—a month ago one could not slip a sheet of thinnest paper under the metatarsal, and now, Sire, even the unpracticed eye is aware of a concavity."

Sister Hyacinthe boomed, "Don't dare to cure them to the point where I will be encouraged to use them."

"She considers only her feet," he said stiffly. "I have my profession and my reputation to think of."

When he was gone and the screen folded and put away, she said, "You know, that pompous little stinker really is curing them, and I dread to think of it."

"One may keep this a secret, Sister," said the king.

"Your color is high, Sire. You have been taking the sun?"

"I've been riding my scooter through the countryside, Sister."

She laughed. "I should like to see the Sun King doing it," she said. "Times are changed, I guess—a motor scooter, and I imagine your ministers are quarreling over the horsepower of their limousines."

"How did you know?" he asked.

"There are things one knows, Sire. For example, I know that you have a problem, that it is a grave problem, and that you have come to me for help in its solution."

"You are very wise," said the king.

"Not wise enough to get out of the chorus before my arches fell."

"But once out, Sister, you took a very long step toward Heaven."

"You are amiable, M'sieur. It may well be that my closeness to Heaven is a by-product. Stumble would be a better word than step. Are you ready to state your problem?"

"I have first to isolate it, Sister. In general it might be stated with the question, 'What is a man to do?'"

"It is not precisely a new problem," she said musingly. "And it usually resolves itself that one does what one is. The first move should be to determine what the man is; that being established, there is very little latitude in what he does."

"One learns so much more easily about other people," said Pippin.

Sister Hyacinthe said, "On leaving the excellent school where Madame was my friend and on taking my place in the Folies, I was troubled about—loss of innocence. Then I discovered that not its loss but the timing of its loss was the problem. My timing was ill-advised, with the result that I had to lose my innocence on several occasions, and after that it was of no importance. But then I was one of many naked girls on a stage—not a king."

"At this moment I feel very naked," said the king.

"Of course you do. It takes time and a certain blunting. But do you know, after a few years I felt much more naked in clothes than without them?"

Pippin said abruptly, "Sister, I am not allowed the time."

"I know," she said. "I'm sorry."

"What shall I do?"

"I don't know what you should do, Sire, but I think I know what you will do."

"You know my dilemma?"

"Only the self-blinded could fail to see it. You will do what you do."

"That's what the old man said. But he was only pulling statues out of the mud. If I am in error, people will suffer—Marie, Clotilde, even France. What would you say, Sister, if a good deed set off an explosion?"

The nun said, "I should say that a good deed may be unwise, but it cannot be evil. It seems to me that the forward history of humans is based on good deeds that exploded—oh! and many were hurt or killed or impoverished, but some of the good remained. I wish—" She paused. "Why not say it? I wish that for the moment I did not wear this—habit."

"Why, Sister?"

"So that I may give you one of the few solaces one human can offer another."

"Thank you, Sister."

"Thank Suzanne, not Hyacinthe. I will ask you to believe, Sire, that at one time Suzanne was not afraid either for her feet or for her soul. Suzanne would have had the courage—and the love."

In the early morning Pippin rode his motor scooter toward Gambais. In his pocket he had a bottle of wine.

He parked his scooter near the road and strolled through the overgrown park, smelling the hint of frost, picking the orange pips from the winter-ready wild-rose vines. A gust of wind dropped curling, darkened leaves from the restless trees on his head and shoulders.

Then he heard a weak shouting ahead of him near the moat and hurried forward until he cleared the edge of the forest and saw three burly youths laughing and wrestling playfully with the ancient. They had the bust of Pan in their arms and they moved toward the moat while the old man tugged helplessly at their jackets and shouted curses at them.

Pippin broke into a run, and then he was in the midst of it. The strong young men turned on the furious king, and then they were rolling and fighting and scratching on the ground, and then the squirming clot went over the edge and down into the dark water of the moat. And still the fight continued until the young men held the bleeding king underwater. He ceased to struggle. Then in fear they clambered, dripping, up the slippery bank and ran, ran in panic and disappeared into the autumn forest.

Pippin gradually came back to consciousness. The ancient had pulled his head and chest out of the water.

"I'm all right, I guess," said the king.

"Don't look it! Them young thugs. I know 'em. I'll go to their people. I'll bring a charge."

"As long as I'm wet already, I might as well dig around in the water for the vase and the Leda and the baby with a shell."

"You'll do no such thing. I got the vase yesterday. You'll come to my place and get dry and warmed up. I got a half-bottle of cognac."

Pippin crawled up the slippery bank. He was covered with green scum like the bust of Pan, one eye was black, and a line of blood ran from his split lip.

In a little shack hidden within the fringe of the forest his friend built up the fire and helped him to remove his clothes and bathed him with a sponge and a bucket of warm water, and dried him with frayed clean rags.

"You look like you been in a cat fight," he said. "Here, take a nip of this. Put this blanket around you. I'll hang your clothes over the stove."

Pippin dug in the pocket of his spongy corduroy jacket for the bottle of wine.

"I brought you this as a present," he said.

The old man held the bottle away from him as far as his arms would reach and squinted at the label.

"Why this—this is—is christening wine—this is wine for a wedding. I don't know if I'll ever have a day again would justify pulling this cork."

"Nonsense," said Pippin. "Open it. I'll help you drink it."

"It not yet the hour of nine?"

"Open it," said the king, and he gathered the blanket about his shoulders.

The ancient drew the cork tenderly. "Now why would you think to bring a wine like this to me?"

"Maybe in celebration of the ones who pull things out."

"Oh! You mean like the statues—"

"Or like me. Drink up! Drink up!"

The old man tasted and smacked his lips. "A wine like this—" he said helplessly. He wiped his lips with his sleeve for fear some extraneous flavor might creep in.

Pippin said, "Last night I thought of something I wanted to ask you. What do you think of the king?"

"Which king?"

"The king—Pippin the Fourth, by the Grace of God Monarch of France."

"Oh! him." And then suspiciously: "What you getting at? I don't want trouble, wine or no wine. Why'd you come to think of it at night?"

"I just wondered. It's only a question—no trouble. Who could give you trouble?"

"You never can tell," the old man said.

"Fill up your glass and tell me. What do you think of him?"

"I've got no politics outside of right here in Gambais. What do I know about the king? He's just the king, I guess. There's kings and then there's not kings, only—"

"Only what?"

"Well, there isn't rightly any kings anymore. Kings? They're like those blasted big lizards, big as a house. They run out. They disappeared, they're ex—ex—"

"Extinct?"

"That's it, extinct. Seems like there wasn't room for them."

"But there is a King of France."

"He's like a play game for children," the old man said. "He's like Father Christmas. He's there, but when you get old enough you don't believe in him anymore. He—well—he's just a dream, like."

"Do you think there will ever be any kings anymore?"

"How should I know? What do you keep picking at me for? You'd think you was related to him." He surveyed the clothes hanging over the stove. "But you ain't."

"Would you know if there was a real king, not just a dream?"

"I guess so."

"How would you know?"

"Well, he'd come riding down the crops on his horses—or there'd be trouble and he'd hang a lot of folks—or he'd say, maybe, 'There's a raft of bad things going on and I'm going to fix them—'" His voice dwindled away. "No, I guess none of them would answer. I know plenty of rich men that do like that, but they ain't kings. I guess there's only one way you'd know for sure."

"What?"

"Well—if they'd take him out and guillotine him I guess you'd be pretty sure he was a king. I guess you would."

Pippin got up and went to the stove and lifted down his damp and steaming clothes from the drying cords.

"They're not dry yet."

"I know—but I must go."

"You going to report me to somebody for something?"

"No," said the king. "You've answered my question. And— by God, I'll do it! A man can't stand being extinct. Perhaps I'll do it badly, but I'll do it."

"What are you talking about? You haven't had that much wine."

Pippin pulled on his clammy clothes. "I'll send you some wine," he said. "I owe it to you."

"For what?"

"You have told me. To be guillotined a man must have done something to make him worthy of the guillotine. The guillotine or—or the Cross requires either a thief or— Thank you, my puller-out-of-things."

The king strode out of the shack and walked rapidly through

the forest to the thicket by the roadside where his scooter was hidden.

In the royal apartment the queen rubbed lemon oil on a polished tabletop.

"How many times must I say that a glass should not be set down without something under it?"

The king put his arms around her and drew her close.

"What are you doing? Pippin, you're wet! Pippin, look at your face—your eye! What have you done?"

"Tripped over the coping and fell in the carp pond."

"You'll never learn to look where you're going. Pippin! Someone might come in— M'sieur—they don't knock."

On one point all ministers, delegates, nobles, and academicians were agreed. The opening of the convention must be regal. Too many of the recently honored had not yet been able to display publicly their robes and feathers, hats, medals, rosettes, and braid. The king was requested to attend the opening in state and deliver a short and tasteful address from the throne. A number of sample speeches were sent to him, based on the cautious sentiments of British royalty.

The King of France should accept the love and support of his subjects, should mention his own love both for his subjects and for the Kingdom of France, should recognize the glorious past and anticipate a glorious future. He should then retire and leave the making of the constitution, or rather of the Code Pippin, to the delegates.

Pippin agreed to this, but then the argument about costumes raged for two hours. The committee was large, and its members insisted on standing, although the sovereign suggested that they sit. Furthermore two elderly noblemen uncomfortably wore their hats, a right their forebears had been granted by Francis I—to remain covered in the presence of the king.

Pippin IV said acidly, "It was my impression and my hope, gentlemen, that this coming deliberation was for the purpose of devising a constitution, a body of laws dealing with ordinary things in the lives of ordinary people. Why is it necessary that we turn it into a costume party reminiscent of those given by South American millionaires in Venice? Why may we all not wear sober clothing of our own time?"

A Socialist and a nobleman fought for the floor and the Socialist won, no less a Socialist than Honnête Jean Veauvache, now Comte des Quatre Chats. M. le Comte replied for the whole committee, as the nodding of heads indicated.

"Your Majesty," he said, "there is nothing ordinary about law. On the contrary, it is a mystical matter, in most minds closely related to religion. And, as the dispensers of holy law find vestments necessary, so do the servants of civil law. Remark, Sire, that our judges preside in gowns and caps. Think of English judges, who require themselves not only to sit in robes and wigs, regardless of the heat of the weather, but even to carry nosegays of flowers, once designed to cover the smell of the people, but not abandoned in a less odoriferous period. And in America, Sire, the most irascibly democratic of nations, where panoply in government is forbidden and where the chief of state is required to be the worst dressed of all—even there, I am told, the ordinary people, feeling robbed, join secret organizations, where regularly they wear crowns and robes and ermine, and speak in rituals of antiquity which give them solemn solace even though they do not understand the words.

"No, Majesty, the common people not only do not want commonness; they will not permit it.

"I ask you to remember Louis Philippe, the so-called Bourgeois King, who dared to walk the streets in ordinary clothing and moreover to carry an umbrella. He was banished from France by an outraged people.

"Finally, Sire, the flower of France will be sitting and their ladies will be in the galleries. They have purchased new robes—even coronets. They are not to be denied the right to wear them. These may seem small things, but actually they are very large and very important. And if to this assembly should come the king, dressed in a two-button suit and a Sulka tie, carrying his papers in a briefcase, I shudder to think of the reaction. Indeed I feel that such a king would be laughed out of office."

The committee was nodding as one man, and when Honnête Jean finished, the members were constrained to applaud.

He was followed by a venerable Academician, a man whose name and whose wisdom are bywords in the world.

"I wish to second the words of Monsieur le Comte," said the master, "but I wish to go one step further. Majesty may do almost anything it wishes save one. The king may not permit himself to be ridiculous. It is the one thing which will inevitably destroy him. In my youth, Sire, it was my good fortune to study under a very learned man, but also a man of huge understanding. At one time he told me the following: 'If,' he said, 'the greatest intellect in the world should be called before the fifty next greatest minds in the world to discuss a problem of such importance that the earth's existence depended on it, and if that greatest man in his preoccupation had neglected to button his fly, the meeting not only would not hear a word he said—it's members would be unable to control their giggles.'"

The king had his pince-nez riding on his forefinger.

"My lords," he said, "I do not wish to be obstructive. Neither have I any desire to inhibit you in your new wardrobes and those of your wives, but at the coronation, in all that stuff, I felt a fool; moreover, I must have looked a fool."

"Not so, Your Majesty," they chorused.

"Well, anyway, I was so hot I couldn't breathe."

Le Comte des Quartre Chats held up his hand again to be recognized.

"It would be sufficient, Sire, if you would appear in the uniform, say, of a Grand Marshal of France."

"But I am not a Grand Marshal."

"The king, Sire, is whatever he wishes to appoint himself."

"But I have no such uniform."

"There are the museums, Sire. Surely Les Invalides can furnish a Grand Marshal's uniform."

The king was silent for a moment, and then he said, "If I agree to this, gentlemen, will you permit that I arrive from Versailles by automobile rather than by the state coach? You don't know how uncomfortable that coach can be."

After a whispered conference it was so agreed, but Honnête Jean said finally, "We, your loyal servants, Sire, would be pleased if during your address—only during—you would permit the purple robe of royalty to be dropped over your shoulders."

"Oh, Lord!" said Pippin. "All right, I'll agree, but only during the speech."

And it was so concluded.

On the afternoon of December 4, while the palace of Versailles was a madhouse of scurrying noblemen, trying on, shortening, lengthening, mending, and walking before mirrors in the robes of their station, the king in his corduroy jacket and crash helmet walked to the guard post at the gate, winked at the captain of the guard, with whom he had struck up a friendship, and passed into his hands a package of Lucky Strikes.

Pippin knew that the captain was in the service of the Minister of Secret Police—but then, he was also in the service of the Socialist party, the British Embassy, and the Peruvian Purchasing Agency, and half-owner of a pâtisserie in Charonne, just off the Boulevard Voltaire. Capitaine Pasmouches reported to each of his clients about all the others, but he genuinely liked the king and he genuinely liked Lucky Strikes.

"This way, M'sieur," he said, and escorted the helmeted and goggled Pippin to the guards' house, where the motor scooter reposed under a tarpaulin. "Will you be going near Charonne, M'sieur?" he asked.

"I can, I suppose," said the king.

"Could you carry a note to my wife at the Pâtisserie Pasmouches?"

"Gladly," said the king. "It's a little out of my way, of course." And as he pocketed the folded paper he said, "Of course if there should be inquiries—"

"I have seen nothing, M'sieur," said the captain. "Even to M'sieur the Minister, I have seen nothing."

The king kicked the starter and mounted the scooter. "It is plain to see that you carry a marshal's baton in your boot, my Captain," he said.

"You are amiable, M'sieur," said Capitaine Pasmouches.

It was very considerably out of his way, but the afternoon was pleasant and sunny, a good day for riding and a relief from the towering nonsense of Versailles. The king presented the note to Madame Pasmouches, who treated him to a cup of coffee and an assortment of petits fours.

After compliments given and taken, the king scooted in the howling traffic of the Place de la Bastille, gunned along the Rue de Rivoli, crossed at the Pont Neuf, and turned into the Rue de Seine.

The shutters of Charles Martel were closed and so was the door. Pippin banged on the door with his fist, and no response came from within. He moved aside and waited patiently until the door opened a crack, then placed his toe firmly in the opening.

Uncle Charlie complained, "Can't a man have privacy even of a gallant nature?"

"I don't believe it," said the king.

"Oh! Come on in. What is it that you want?"

The king slipped into the darkened gallery and saw that the walls were bare and that large wooden boxes stood about, packed and ready to be nailed shut.

"You are going on a trip, my Uncle?"

"Yes."

"Won't you invite me to sit down? Why are you angry
with me?"

"Come in, then. The chairs are covered. You will have to sit
on a box."

"You are running away?"

"I don't trust you," said Uncle Charlie. "I can put two and
two together. You're up to something. And you will lose, my
child. I don't see any reason why I also should lose because of
your foolishness."

"I came for advice."

"Then I'll give it to you. Go and be a king in a proper way
and stop sticking your nose into business and—and government, where it isn't wanted. That's my advice to you. If you
would take it, I could unpack."

"You told me once that I was a patsy—a royal patsy. A patsy
is a kind of pawn, is it not, something to be used as long as possible and then lost without grieving?"

"I suppose so. But when a pawn tries to do the work of
government—then the pawn is a fool."

Pippin seated himself on a crate. "Will you give me a glass of
brandy?"

"I don't have any."

"What is that bottle I see back there?"

"That is marc."

"Perhaps, then, a thimbleful of marc. You must be terrified,
my Uncle, to have lost your courtesy."

"I am terrified. And I'm afraid of you."

The king said, "A king can move one square forward, back-
ward, sideways, aslant, but a patsy—or a pawn—only ahead.
Thank you, Uncle Charlie, won't you have one with me? Won't
you drink my health? Must your sense of guilty disloyalty
make you hate me?"

Uncle Charlie sighed very deeply. "I *am* ashamed," he said at
last. "However, my shame will not change my course. I am going to America for a while, until—until it blows over. I don't
know exactly what you intend to do, but I know it is disaster.
And you are right about one thing. There is no excuse for dis-
courtesy. Forgive me!"

"I know how you must feel, but I have thought deeply about this, my Uncle. A king is an anachronism—a king doesn't really exist."

"What do you propose?"

"Simply to make a few suggestions, based on my observations."

"They will guillotine you. They don't want suggestions."

"That is one thing I have learned. A king must be worthy of the guillotine. And maybe one or two of my suggestions might take root."

"I've always hated martyrs."

Pippin drank his marc and shuddered. "I'm not a martyr, Uncle Charlie. A martyr trades something he has for something he wants. I am not ambitious."

"What are you then—mischievous?"

"Perhaps. Or maybe only curious. And surely not brave."

"I used to think I knew you. How about Marie? How about Clotilde? Have you no feeling for them?"

"That is what I came to see you about, to ask you to look after them—that is, if an occasion should arise."

"How about yourself?"

"I am being dramatic. I think the time and my office require it. I can take care of myself."

"You plan to do this thing tomorrow?"

"Yes. And I would be glad if you invited Madame and Clotilde to visit you tomorrow—perhaps you could take them on a little trip into the country. Perhaps the young Mr. Johnson might assist you. He has an automobile. A weekend on the Loire. There is a beautiful little inn at Sancerre. But I imagine you know it."

"I know it."

"Will you do it?"

Uncle Charlie cursed filthily for several seconds.

"Then you will do it!" said the king.

"It's a trick! You think you have the right to maneuver me because we are related. It is a detestable piece of blackmail."

"Then that is settled!" said Pippin. "Thank you, Uncle Charlie. I don't anticipate trouble and so I anticipate trouble." He arose from the crate.

"Oh, have another drink," said Uncle Charlie. "I think I have just a few drops of brandy."

"You make me very happy," said the king. "I knew I could depend on you."

"Merde!" said Uncle Charlie.

Half a mile from the Palace of Versailles, Pippin turned his scooter off the road and into the forest. He pushed it over the deep carpet of fallen leaves far back from the highway. In the lee of an outcropping of stone he dogpaddled the fallen autumn leaves away, then put his scooter in the hollow, and covered it with leaves. He piled a few wind-fallen branches on top to hold the leaves in place. Then he walked out of the forest and continued on foot.

At the gate he told the captain, "I delivered your letter. Madame says to tell you she will take care of it. She would like you to telephone to Ars et Fils and tell them, so they may tell her when you can come in. I must say her cakes are delicious."

"Thank you, M'sieur. Where is your machine?"

The king shrugged. "I had a small accident. It is being repaired. A kind tourist brought me nearly here. Naturally I did not want him to—"

"I understand, M'sieur. There has been no inquiry."

"I guess they're all too busy with themselves," said the king.

At dinner the queen said, "Your Uncle Charles has asked Clotilde and me to drive to Sancerre. I don't think this is a time—"

"On the contrary, my dear. I shall be busy at the convention. And you need a holiday. You have worked hard and long."

"But I have a million things—"

"Quite between us, my dear, I think it would be good to take Clotilde away from Paris for a few days. Just as a matter of policy, you know—she is talking too much to the newspapers. Sancerre, eh? I remember it as a lovely little town with a great wine if you can get any of it."

"I'll think about it," said the queen. "I have so much on my mind. I wonder, Pippin, whether I should tell you now—the agents absolutely refuse to terminate the lease at Number One Avenue de Marigny. They insist that a lease is a lease, no matter what the government."

"Perhaps we can sublet it later."

"Just one more thing to worry about," said the queen. "You know how tenants are. And most of my mother's furniture is still there."

"You need a little holiday, my dear. You've had too many responsibilities."

"I wonder what I should take."

"Just simple things for motoring and a warm coat. It may be quite chilly on the river this time of year. I wish I could go with you."

The queen looked at him speculatively. "I don't like to leave you just at this time."

He took her hand and turned it palm upward and kissed it. "It's the perfect time," he said. "I'll be so busy with the convention, you would not even see me."

"Perhaps you're right," she said. "So much talk and politics buzzing around. I'm tired of the nobility, my dear. I'm bored with politics. Sometimes I wish we still lived in our little stable-house. That is a very pleasant neighborhood. But the concierge is impossible."

"I know," said the king, "but what can you expect of Alsatians?"

"There you have it," said the queen. "Alsatians—provincials, I say. Only interested in their tight little lives. Provincials! Do you think I should take my fur coat?"

"I strongly advise it," said the king.

Everyone has seen photographs of the historic opening of the convention to deliberate the Code Pippin. Every newspaper and magazine in the world printed at least one version of it. The half-circle of rows of seats, filled with robed delegates, the speakers' rostrum and the high, thronelike chair of the Chief

Minister, whose duty it was to control and govern the proceedings.

The photographs show the eager faces of the delegates in every manner of ceremonial costume; the galleries filled to overflowing with ladies, also costumed and coroneted; the guards at the doorways in slashed doublets and carrying halberds. Not visible in the pictures are the bales of papers, the mountains of books of precedent, the ledgers, briefcases, even small filing cabinets which rested on the floor among the delegates' feet, containing the weapons wherewith each party planned to save France by aggrandizing itself.

The meeting convened at three P.M. December 5, and it was agreed that after the address from the throne it should recess until the next day. The king was neither invited to nor wanted at the subsequent meetings. At the end he was expected to place his royal signature on the Code, preferably without reading it.

It will be remembered that the Duc des Troisfronts had made the first demand for the return of the monarchy. It was therefore considered only proper that he should announce the king, in spite of his cleft palate.

At 3:15 the Chief Minister raised the royal gavel, actually a wooden replica of the hammer from which Charles Martel took his name.

The hammer crashed nobly down three times. From the entrance to the right of the rostrum the halberdiers wheeled inward, opened the double doors, and presented their arms.

The Duc des Troisfronts entered. He was scaled like a lizard with orders and decorations, while a toupee which was an integral part of his coronet gave him an alert look—a little like the March Hare. He advanced to the rostrum and glanced about in panic. Academician Poitin of the Royal Academy of Music rapped three times with his baton, and six trumpeters in tabards raised six-foot straight trumpets from which hung the royal arms. M. Poitin gave them a downbeat, and they blew a fanfare which seemed to rock the great room.

The Duc des Troisfronts struggled for breath. "Hentulmeh. I hive you the Hing of Fhance!"

From the gallery the Duchess was heard to break into applause.

Again the fanfare.

Again the halberdiers swung open the double doors—and Pippin entered.

By no stretch of imagination could he have been thought to have either a military figure or carriage. The marshal's uniform was a mistake. Moreover, the uniform—rented from a theatrical costumer—had at the last moment been discovered to be far too large. The tunic had been made to fit by a row of safety pins up the back. Nothing could be done about the crotch of the trousers, which, even though the waistband was high on his chest, still dangled halfway to his knees. The purple velvet cape with edging of ermine hung from his shoulders and was followed by two pages delegated to control it. They did their best, and when the king reached the rostrum and turned they brought the trailing ends of the train inward to try to conceal his pants, so that he arose out of its folds like the stamen of a lily.

The king placed the manuscript of his address on the rostrum. His hands wandered to his breast, searched frantically amongst the great stars and orders. His glasses were not there. He remembered putting his pince-nez and the ribbon down while his tunic was being pinned up the back. He spoke to one of the boys, who dashed out through the side entrance, knocking a halberd from a guard's hand.

Meanwhile Le Maître Poitin, who after all had been fifty years in the theater, signaled the trumpeters to break into the traditional hunting call whose triumphant theme, "There goes the fox," puts a strain on the versatility of the straight trumpet.

While this brilliant improvisation continued, the page returned and handed the king his pince-nez. Pippin bent over his pages, written in the precise but minute hand of the mathematician.

Pippin reach his speech exactly as though he was reading a speech. His voice had no rise and fall. His points were made with no underlining and no declamation.

No one could find any fault with the opening statement:

"My Lords, and my People—

"We, Pippin, King of France by right of blood and by further authority of election, do hold that this land has been singularly favored by God with richness of soil and geniality of climate, while its people are endowed with intelligence and talent above many others—"

At this point applause broke out, which caused him to look up, remove his pince-nez, and lose his place.

When the noise had subsided he replaced his pince-nez and bent over the tiny handwriting.

"Let's see. M-mmm—here it is—talent above many others. When we assumed the crown, we made a careful study of the nation, its riches, its failures, and its potentials. Not only did we study available statistics but also we went out among the people, not in our royal character but on the level of the people themselves—"

He paused and looked up and remarked conversationally, "If that seems romantic to some of you, I ask you how else I could have found out."

He went back to his manuscript.

A slight uneasiness crept into the great gathering.

"We found," he said pedantically—"we found that the power, the products, the comforts, the profits, and the opportunities of our nation deserve a wider distribution than they now have."

Right and Left Centrists looked at one another in consternation.

"We believe that changes, programs, and some restrictions are necessary to the end that our people may live in comfort and peace and that the genius of the French, which once lighted the world, may be rekindled."

During the time it took him to turn a page there was a little pattering of scattered handclapping. The delegates restlessly moved their feet among their books and briefcases.

Pippin continued.

"The People of France have created a king. It is not only the nature but the duty of a king to rule. Where a president may suggest, a king must order—otherwise his office is meaningless and his kingdom does not exist.

"We therefore order and decree that the Code you are creating shall contain the following. . . ."

And then the bomb exploded.

The first section dealt with taxes—to be kept as low as possible and to be collected from all.

The second, wages—to be keyed to profits and to move up and down with the cost of living.

Prices—to be strictly controlled against manipulation.

Housing—existing housing to be improved and new construction to be undertaken with supervision as to quality and rents.

The fifth section called for a reorganization of government to the end that it perform its functions with the least expenditure of money and personnel.

The sixth considered public health insurance and retirement pensions.

The seventh ordered the breakup of great land holdings to restore the wasted earth to productivity.

"To the great three words I want to add a fourth," he said, "so that henceforth the motto of the French shall be 'Liberty, Equality, Fraternity, *and* Opportunity.'"

The king, his head still down, waited for applause, and when none came he looked out over the thunderstruck gathering. The delegates were hypnotized with horror. They stared glassily back at the king. They seemed scarcely to breathe.

Pippin IV had planned to bow at this point and to leave with dignity on the heels of his applause, but there was only aching silence. Uproar he could have understood. He had even prepared himself for denunciation, but the silence held him and confused him. He took off his pince-nez and mounted it on his forefinger.

"I meant every word I said," he began uneasily. "I have really seen France, France which has survived three invasions, two occupations in three generations, and emerged whole and strong and free. I tell you what an enemy could not do to us we are doing to ourselves, like greedy, destructive children throwing cake at a birthday party."

And suddenly he was angry—coldly angry.

"I didn't ask to be king," he said hoarsely. "I begged not to be king. And you didn't want a king. You wanted a patsy."

Then he shouted, "But you elected a king, and by God you've got a king—or a gigantic joke."

Delegates cleared their throats, took off their glasses and polished them.

"I know as well as you do that the time for kings is past," he said quietly. "Royalty is extinct and its place is taken by boards of directors. What I have tried to do is to help you make the leap, for you are not one thing or the other. I am going to leave you now to your deliberations. You have my orders—but, whether you obey them or not, try to be worthy of our beautiful nation."

The king bowed slightly and turned to walk toward the door, but an open-mouthed page was standing on the edge of his purple and ermine-collared cape. It ripped from his shoulders and fell to the floor, exposing the row of safety pins up the back of his tunic, and the baggy crotch of the trousers flopping between his knees.

Strain in children and adults opens two avenues of relief—laughter or tears—and either is equally accessible. The safety pins did it.

Beginning with a snigger in the front benches, it spread to giggles, and then to hysterical laughter. Delegates pounded the backs of the delegates in front of them and honked and roared and wiped their eyes. Thus they channeled the shock the king's message had given them, the shock and the terror and their own deep sense of guilt.

Pippin could hear the laughter through the closed doors. He removed the baggy pants and hung them on a chair. He put on his dark blue suit with its pin stripe and tied his black silk knitted tie.

Quietly he went out a rear entrance and walked around the

building and stood in the crowd gathered at the noble marble entrance. People said, "What's all the noise? What's going on in there?"

The king moved slowly away from the excited people. He walked in the streets a while, looked in windows. At a music store he bought a small cheap harmonica, and, concealing it in his hand, he blew a chord on it now and then. He walked down to the Seine embankment and watched the eternal fishermen with their filament lines and bread-crumb bait.

And then, because the days were growing short, he bought a ticket on the Versailles bus and went home. He wandered about in the empty royal apartments.

He turned out the lights and pulled a chair to the leaded window overlooking the gardens. He took the harmonica from his pocket and tried it timidly. In an hour he had worked out the scale. In two hours he produced a slow and labored "Auprès de ma blonde, qu'il fait bon, fait bon, fait bon."

Pippin smiled, sitting in the dark. The palace was quiet. He played "Frère Jacques" slowly but accurately from beginning to end. The carp burped loudly in the fish ponds.

Meanwhile, telegraph and radio transoceanic telephones staggered under the weight of traffic.

Dark-suited men sped to chancelleries. Private and secret wires went into action. The State Department in Washington froze French assets in the United States.

Luxembourg mobilized.

Monaco closed its borders and its soldiers tore the flowers from their rifle barrels.

A Soviet submarine was sighted in San Francisco Bay.

A squadron of Soviet destroyers gave chase to an American submarine in the Gulf of Finland.

Sweden and Switzerland declared their neutrality while putting themselves in a position of defense.

England growled and grumbled with delight and suggested that the royal family could find traditional sanctuary in London.

Paris was shuttered. Students from the Sorbonne swarmed up the Eiffel Tower and ripped down the royal standard and raised the Tricolor among the wind gauges.

At Suze-sous-Cure, the populace, led by the chief of police, burned the town hall, whereupon the police station was burned by the same populace under the leadership of the mayor.

Falaise in Normandy rounded up all strangers and guarded them.

At Le Puy bonfires burned on the pinnacles.

Marseille rioted courteously and looted with discrimination.

The Pope offered arbitration.

In Paris the gendarmes helped the rioters build barricades, using police hurdles.

The warehouses up-Seine were broken open, and wine barrels rumbled over the cobbles.

Partisans howled with enthusiasm and revolt. Right Centrists posted ink-wet bills saying TO THE BASTILLE.

The American ambassador denounced revolution.

The Kremlin, China, the satellites, and Egypt telegraphed congratulations to the heroic People's Republic of France.

In the dark and quiet room at Versailles, Pippin tried to play the "Memphis Blues" and found he had no sharps and flats on his instrument. He moved on to "Home on the Range," which requires none, and was so intent on his work that he did not hear the soft knocking on the door.

Sister Hyacinthe opened the door, looked in, and saw the king silhouetted against the window. Her low laughter made him stop his playing and peer around at her. She looked like a great black bird against the painted wall.

"It is good to have a second trade," she said.

The king stood up awkwardly and knocked the moisture from the harmonica against the palm of his hand. "I didn't hear you, Sister."

"No. You were too busy, Sire."

He said a little stiffly, "One finds oneself doing silly things."

"Perhaps not silly, Sire. The mind seeks curious retreats. I did not know you were here. Nearly everyone else has gone."

"Where have they gone, Sister?"

"Some went to save themselves, but most have simply gone to Paris to see the fireworks. They are drawn to activity as insects are drawn to light. I myself am leaving, Sire. My Superior has ordered me to return. I am afraid, Sire, that your short reign is over. I am told that all France is in revolt."

"I was not ready to think about it," said Pippin. "I suppose I have failed."

"I don't know," said the nun. "I have read your remarks to the convention. They were bold remarks, Sire. Yes, I imagine that you have failed, you personally, but I wonder whether your words have failed. I remember another who failed—whose words we live by." She placed a small bundle on the table beside him. "A present for you, Sire, the time-honored disguise."

"What is it?"

"One of my habits, a nun's dress, the traditional means of escape. I see no reason for either hemlock or cross."

Pippin said, "Is it that bad? Are they really so furious?"

"I don't know," said Sister Hyacinthe. "You have caught them in error. It will be very difficult for them to forgive you. Your words will be thorns in every future government. You will haunt them. Perhaps they sense that."

"I want to find Marie," he said. "I thought perhaps she would come here."

"Maybe she will—or maybe she is not able to get back. I understand there is an uproar in Paris. When they have exhausted the fun in Paris the rioters may come here. If you intend to go, I suggest that you go tonight."

"Without Marie—without Clotilde?"

"I don't think they are in as much danger as you, Sire. If you will put on this habit, you can go with me. My convent will conceal you until it is safe to cross the frontier."

"I don't want to cross the frontier, Sister. I really don't think I am so important that they will want my life."

"Your Majesty," the nun said, "they may well be afraid of each other. Every group may feel that the others might join you."

"I can't believe it," said the king. "The kingdom was a myth—it didn't exist. And the king? What is he but a kind of national joke? I don't believe they will dignify the kingship with murder."

"I don't know," she said uncertainly. "I really don't know."

He said, "If I escape or try to, I will be making myself important enough to kill. I've often wondered what would have happened if Louis the Sixteenth had not tried to escape—if he had walked alone and unguarded to the Jeu de Paume."

"You are brave, Sire."

"No, Sister, I am not brave. Perhaps I am stupid, but I am not brave. I do not want to be a sacrifice. I want my little house, my wife, and my telescope—nothing more. If they had not forced me to be king I would not have been forced to be kingly. It was a series of psychological accidents."

"I wish I could be sure that you were safe. But I must go, M'sieur. Do you know that so-and-so has cured my feet? I may not forgive him for that. You will not come with me?"

"No, Sister."

"Give me your hand!"

Sister Hyacinthe bowed over his hand and kissed it. "Goodby—Your Majesty."

When he looked up she had gone, so silently that not even the parquetry had protested.

Pippin put the still warm harmonica against his lips and played very slowly, *do-re-mi-fa-sol-la*— He missed on the *ti*, went back and corrected it, and completed with *do*.

He went down the circular staircase to the garden. His footsteps sounded loud on the gravel. He strolled around to the great entrance and for a time he could not see that any guard was posted. Then a match was lighted and he saw a single guardsman seated on the ground, his back against the kiosk, his rifle leaning against the wall. The king approached.

"Are you all alone?"

"They all went to Paris," the guard complained. "It isn't fair. Why should I be picked to stay—and told—and ordered to stay? My service record will show that I have been a good soldier."

"Would you like a Lucky Strike?"

"Do you have one?"

"You may have the whole package."

The guard stood up suspiciously. "Who are you?"

"I am the king."

"Pardon, Sire. I didn't recognize you. I beg pardon."

"What is going on in Paris?"

"That's just it. I don't know. Great doings. They say riots and all such like—maybe even looting—and here I have to sit and miss it all."

"It doesn't seem fair," said Pippin. "Why don't you go?"

"Oh, I couldn't do that. I would be court-martialed, and I have a family. I have to think of them. The captain ordered—"

Pippin said, "Do you believe that I outrank the captain?"

"Certainly, Sire."

"Then I relieve you of your duty."

"It can't be just word of mouth. What proof do I have?"

"Do you have a flashlight?"

"Of course, Sire."

"Lend it to me." Pippin went into the kiosk to the little shelf with its pad and pencil. "What is your name?" he asked.

"Vautin, Sergeant Vautin, Sire."

Pippin wrote on the pad, "Sergeant Vautin is hereby relieved of duty and authorized to begin furlough of two weeks beginning at—" "What time is it?"

"Twelve and twenty minutes, Sire."

Pippin continued: "at 12:20 A.M." He filled in the date and signed it "Pippin IV, King of France, Commander-in-Chief of All Armed Forces." He handed the order and the flashlight to the soldier.

Sergeant Vautin put the light on the paper and read it carefully.

"I can't see who could find fault with that, Sire. But who is to guard the gate?"

"I'll keep an eye on it."

"Don't you want to go to the riots, Sire?"

"Not particularly," said Pippin.

He watched the soldier ride happily away on his bicycle and then he sat down with his back against the kiosk.

The night was chilly but brilliant with stars, and it was very quiet. No automobiles moved on the highways. Far away the lights of Paris were reflected in a glow against the sky. The great palace was dark behind him. He thought to himself that no night had been so still here for fifty years at least.

And then he heard the distant hum of a motor, then saw the lights of a speeding car. It screeched to a stop at the gates—a Buick convertible. The headlights blinded Pippin sitting against the kiosk.

Tod Johnson leaped out of the car and left the motor running. "Hurry up, sir. Get in."

Clotilde called from the car, "Hurry, Father!"

Tod said, "You can put on some of my clothes in the car. We'll get to the Channel by daylight."

Pippin got slowly to his feet. "What is it you intend to do?"

"We're going to try to get across the Channel."

"Is it so bad, then?"

"You don't know, sir. Paris is a mess. You've been deposed, sir. They're yelling for the Republic. If I didn't have an American car we wouldn't have gotten through."

Pippin asked, "Where is Madame?"

"I don't know, sir. She was supposed to go with Uncle Charlie, but she disappeared."

"And where is Uncle Charlie?"

"He went south. He's going to try to cross into Portugal. Come on, sir! Hurry!!"

"You aren't in any danger," Pippin said. "What happened?"

"You didn't listen to what I told you," said Tod. "You didn't have the money and the proxies. You didn't even have the stockholders."

Pippin walked to the car. "Are you all right, Clotilde?"

"I guess so."

"Where will you go?"

"To Hollywood," she said. "Don't forget, I'm an artiste."

"I had forgotten," he said. And to Tod, "You will take care of her?"

"Sure, but come on—get in! Don't worry about anything. Maybe you'd like to learn the chicken business. And you can write articles. They all do. You've got to get away, now, sir. Here, I've got a bottle of brandy. Have a drink."

Pippin took a swallow from the bottle. And suddenly he laughed.

"Don't be upset," said Tod. "We'll get you through."

"I'm not upset," said Pippin Héristal. "I was just thinking about Julius Caesar. He did it once. With five legions he surrounded Vercingetorix at Alesia and he pacified Gaul."

"Maybe Gaul doesn't want to be pacified," said Tod.

The king was silent for a moment and then he said, "That seems to be the truth. And so perhaps even Caesar didn't do it. Maybe Gaul can only be pacified by Gaul."

"Do hurry, Father," said the subdued Clotilde. "You don't know what it's like."

The king said, "Take care of her—as much as anyone can take care of anyone."

"Come along, sir."

"No," said Pippin. "I am not going. I think in a very little while they will forget me."

"They'll kill you, sir."

"I don't think so," said the king. "I really don't think so. And besides, I can't leave Marie. I wonder where she could have gone? You're sure she isn't with Uncle Charlie?"

"No. The last we saw her was in Sancerre. She went shopping with a basket on her arm. Won't you get in?"

Pippin said, "This is probably my last act as king. These are my orders. You will proceed to a Channel port. You will do your best to find a boat to take you and Clotilde to England. These are your orders, Tod. See that you carry them out."

"But—"

"You have your orders," said the king. "Grant me the final courtesy of obeying them."

He watched the Buick move away and then he strolled back to the palace to find his corduroy jacket and his crash helmet.

It was during that night that the delegates constituted themselves a National Assembly. They proclaimed the Republic. The Tricolor rose on public buildings.

The gendarmerie moved to put a stop to looting. The banks were declared closed for the time being.

M. Sonnet, to great applause, asked M. Magot to form a coalition government. The king was declared deposed and out-lawed.

M. Magot was able to form a government in a few hours. It will be remembered that the coalition government lasted until February third of the following year.

The motor scooter ran out of gasoline in the Bois de Boulogne, and Pippin left it leaning against a tree and continued on foot. It was dawn when he turned off the Champs Elysées into the Avenue de Marigny.

From out of the shadows a gendarme moved to intercept him. "You have your card of identity, M'sieur?"

Pippin brought out his wallet and handed over his card. The gendarme studied it and said, "Pippin Héristal. Why, I remember you, M'sieur. You live at Number One."

"That is correct," said Pippin.

"There's been looting," the gendarme observed. "I didn't recognize you in the helmet. Have you been on a trip, M'sieur?"

"Yes," said Pippin, "quite a long trip."

The gendarme saluted. "Everything seems quiet now," he said.

"Will you have a cigarette?"

"Thank you. Ah! a Lucky Strike."

"Keep the package," said Pippin. He winked. "I've been out of the country."

The gendarme smiled. "I understand, M'sieur." And he put the package in his pocket under his cape.

Pippin had to ring the bell endlessly before the concierge shuffled bleary-eyed and ill-tempered to open the iron gate for him.

"A strange time to be coming in," he muttered.

Pippin placed a bill in his hand. "It's a long trip from Strasbourg."

"You have come from Strasbourg?"

"Well, in one jump from Nancy."

"I myself am from Lunéville. How does the country look?"

"They had a great harvest. The geese looked fine and fat. And they say the wine—"

"I've heard—I've heard. But did you hear how the elections in Lunéville came out? That is a very important thing. You see, the mayoralty has been held—" He closed his fist in front of him. "It is time for change—everyone feels that. Everyone, that is, but—" He tightened his fist again.

Pippin said, "I will have to trouble you to open my door— my keys—"

"But Madame is in. You have only to ring. And what a turning out she's given it. Carry this, carry that. What a fury! Now the party in Lunéville that has held it in a grip—"

Pippin said, "Good night, M'sieur. I will want to hear another time. It's a long ride from Nancy."

He crossed the courtyard to the entrance of the stablehouse. He took off his crash helmet and brushed back his hair with his fingers—and finally he laid his finger on the ivory button of the bell.

"Steinbeck shaped a geography of conscience" —Don DeLillo

The Grapes of Wrath
Introduction by Robert DeMott
This Pulitzer Prize–winning epic of the Great Depression follows the western movement of one family and a nation in search of work and human dignity.   *ISBN 0-14-018640-9*

East of Eden
Introduction by David Wyatt
The masterpiece of Steinbeck's later years, *East of Eden* is the powerful and vastly ambitious novel that is both family saga and a modern retelling of the book of Genesis.   *ISBN 0-14-018639-5*

Of Mice and Men
Introduction by Susan Shillinglaw
A parable about commitment, loneliness, hope, and loss, *Of Mice and Men* remains one of America's most widely read and beloved novels.
                    ISBN 0-14-018642-5

Cannery Row
Introduction by Susan Shillinglaw
Steinbeck's tough but loving portrait evokes the lives of Monterey's vital laboring class and their emotional triumph over the bleak existence of life in *Cannery Row*.   *ISBN 0-14-018737-5*

The Pearl
Introduction by Linda Wagner-Martin with Drawings by José Clemente Orozco
The diver Kino believes that his discovery of a beautiful pearl means the promise of a better life for his impoverished family. His fall from innocence is one of Steinbeck's most moving stories about the American dream.   *ISBN 0-14-018738-3*

Travels with Charley in Search of America
Introduction by Jay Parini
In September 1960, Steinbeck and his poodle, Charley, embarked on a journey across America. A picaresque tale, this chronicle of their trip meanders along scenic backroads and speeds along anonymous super-highways, moving from small towns to growing cities to glorious wilderness oases.   *ISBN 0-14-018741-3*

The Portable John Steinbeck
Edited by Pascal Covici, Jr.
This grand sampling of Steinbeck's most important works includes two complete novels, *Of Mice and Men* and *The Red Pony*, as well as excerpts from many of his other books, short stories, and his 1962 Nobel Prize Acceptance Speech.   *ISBN 0-14-015002-1*

America and Americans and Selected Nonfiction
Edited by Susan Shillinglaw and Jackson J. Benson
This original new collection brings together for the first time more than fifty of Steinbeck's finest essays and journalistic pieces, along with the complete text of his last-published and long-out-of-print *America and Americans*.   *ISBN 0-14-243741-7*

Burning Bright
Written as a play in story form, this novel traces the story of a man ignorant of his own sterility, a wife who commits adultery to give her husband a child, the father of that child, and the outsider whose actions affect them all.   *ISBN 0-14-018742-1*

Cup of Gold
Steinbeck's first novel, and the only historical novel he ever wrote, brings to life the exciting, violent adventures of the infamous pirate Henry Morgan.   *ISBN 0-14-018743-X*

In Dubious Battle
Introduction and Notes by Warren French
This powerful social novel, set in the California apple country, is a story of labor unrest in the migrant community and the search for identity of its protagonist, young Jim Nolan.   *ISBN 0-14-018641-7*

The Log from the Sea of Cortez
Introduction by Richard Astro
This exciting day-by-day account of Steinbeck's trip to the Gulf of California with biologist Ed Ricketts, drawn from the longer *Sea of Cortez*, is a wonderful combination of science, philosophy, and high-spirited adventure.   *ISBN 0-14-018744-8*

The Long Valley
Introduction by John H. Timmerman
First published in 1938, this collection of stories set in the rich farmland of the Salinas Valley includes the O. Henry Prize-winning story "The Murder," as well as one of Steinbeck's most famous short works, "The Snake."   *ISBN 0-14-018745-6*

The Moon is Down
Introduction by Donald V. Coers
In this masterful tale set in Norway during World War II, Steinbeck explores the effects of invasion on both the conquered and the conquerors. As he delves into the emotions of the German commander and the Norwegian traitor, and depicts the spirited patriotism of the Norwegian underground, Steinbeck uncovers profound, often unsettling truths about war—and about human nature. *ISBN 0-14-018746-4*

Once There Was a War
Steinbeck's dispatches filed from the front lines during World War II vividly evoke the human side of the war. *ISBN 0-14-018747-2*

The Pastures of Heaven
Introduction and Notes by James Nagel
Each of these interconnected tales is devoted to a family living in a fertile valley on the outskirts of Monterey, California, and the effects, either intentional or unwitting, that one family has on all of them.
ISBN 0-14-018748-0

The Red Pony
Introduction by John Seelye
This cycle of coming-of-age stories tells of a spirited adolescent boy whose encounters with birth and death teach him about loss and profound emptiness, instead of giving him the more conventional hero's pragmatic "maturity." *ISBN 0-14-018739-1*

A Russian Journal
With Photographs by Robert Capa
Introduction by Susan Shillinglaw
First published in 1948, *A Russian Journal* is a remarkable memoir and unique historical document that records the writer and acclaimed war photographer's journey through Cold War Russia.
ISBN 0-14-118019-6

The Short Reign of Pippin IV
Steinbeck's only work of political satire turns the French Revolution upside down, creating the hilarious characters of the motley royal court of King Pippin. *ISBN 0-14-018749-9*

Sweet Thursday
Returning to the scene of *Cannery Row*—the weedy lot and junk heaps and flophouses of Monterey, California—Steinbeck once more brings to life the denizens of a netherworld of laughter and tears, from Fauna, new headmistress of the local brothel, to Hazel, a bum whose mother must have wanted a daughter. *ISBN 0-14-018750-2*

To a God Unknown
Introduction and Notes by Robert DeMott
Set in familiar Steinbeck territory, *To a God Unknown* is a mystical tale, exploring one man's attempt to control the forces of nature and, ultimately, to understand the ways of God. *ISBN 0-14-018751-0*

Tortilla Flat
Introduction by Thomas Fensch
Adopting the structure and themes of the Arthurian legend, Steinbeck created a "Camelot" on a shabby hillside above Monterey on the California coast and peopled it with a colorful band of knights. As Steinbeck chronicles their thoughts and emotions, temptations and lusts, he spins a tale as compelling, and ultimately as touched by sorrow, as the famous legends of the *Round Table*. *ISBN 0-14-018740-5*

The Wayward Bus
In this imaginative and unsentimental chronicle of a bus traveling California's back roads, Steinbeck creates a vivid assortment of characters, all running away from their shattered dreams but hoping that they are running toward the promise of a future. *ISBN 0-14-018752-9*

The Winter of Our Discontent
Ethan Hawley works as a clerk in the grocery store owned by an Italian immigrant. His wife is restless, and his teenaged children are hungry for the tantalizing material comforts he cannot provide. Then one day, in a moment of moral crisis, Ethan decides to take a holiday from his own scrupulous standards. *ISBN 0-14-018753-7*

John Steinbeck, Writer: A Biography
Jackson J. Benson
"The definitive biography of John Steinbeck . . . A book rich in detail, in anecdote, in literary criticism . . . Benson's book is a milestone."
—*San Francisco Chronicle* *ISBN 0-14-014417-X*

Winner of the PEN-West USA Award for Nonfiction

CLICK ON A CLASSIC
www.penguinclassics.com

The world's greatest literature at your fingertips

Constantly updated information on more than a thousand titles,
from Icelandic sagas to ancient Indian epics, Russian drama to
Italian romance, American greats to African masterpieces

❀

The latest news on recent additions to the list, updated
editions, and specially commissioned translations

❀

Original essays by leading writers

❀

A wealth of background material, including biographies
of every classic author from Aristotle to Zamyatin, plot
synopses, readers' and teachers' guides, useful Web links

❀

Online desk and examination copy assistance for academics

❀

Trivia quizzes, competitions, giveaways, news on
forthcoming screen adaptations

FOR THE BEST IN PAPERBACKS, LOOK FOR THE

In every corner of the world, on every subject under the sun, Penguin represents quality and variety—the very best in publishing today.

For complete information about books available from Penguin—including Penguin Classics and Puffins—and how to order them, write to us at the appropriate address below. Please note that for copyright reasons the selection of books varies from country to country.

In the United States: Please write to *Penguin Group (USA), P.O. Box 12289 Dept. B, Newark, New Jersey 07101-5289* or call 1-800-788-6262.

In the United Kingdom: Please write to *Dept. EP, Penguin Books Ltd, Bath Road, Harmondsworth, West Drayton, Middlesex UB7 0DA.*

In Canada: Please write to *Penguin Books Canada Ltd, 90 Eglinton Avenue East, Suite 700, Toronto, Ontario M4P 2Y3.*

In Australia: Please write to *Penguin Books Australia Ltd, P.O. Box 257, Ringwood, Victoria 3134.*

In New Zealand: Please write to *Penguin Books (NZ) Ltd, Private Bag 102902, North Shore Mail Centre, Auckland 10.*

In India: Please write to *Penguin Books India Pvt Ltd, 11 Panchsheel Shopping Centre, Panchsheel Park, New Delhi 110 017.*

In the Netherlands: Please write to *Penguin Books Netherlands bv, Postbus 3507, NL-1001 AH Amsterdam.*

In Germany: Please write to *Penguin Books Deutschland GmbH, Metzlerstrasse 26, 60594 Frankfurt am Main.*

In Spain: Please write to *Penguin Books S. A., Bravo Murillo 19, 1° B, 28015 Madrid.*

In Italy: Please write to *Penguin Italia s.r.l., Via Benedetto Croce 2, 20094 Corsico, Milano.*

In France: Please write to *Penguin France, Le Carré Wilson, 62 rue Benjamin Baillaud, 31500 Toulouse.*

In Japan: Please write to *Penguin Books Japan Ltd, Kaneko Building, 2-3-25 Koraku, Bunkyo-Ku, Tokyo 112.*

In South Africa: Please write to *Penguin Books South Africa (Pty) Ltd, Private Bag X14, Parkview, 2122 Johannesburg.*

Printed in the United States
by Baker & Taylor Publisher Services